Susan Super Sleuth

by
William Ettridge

Illustrations by Laura Piotrowski

Potlatch Publications Limited,
One Duke Street,
Hamilton, Ontario.

ISBN 0-919676-18-9

Printed in Canada.

Table of Contents

Susan Super Sleuth and
The Kidnap Caper

ere we are at last!'' Susan unsnapped her seat belt as the aircraft gently came to a stop, the forward exit door exactly in line with the covered ramp which slowly reached out like a huge elephant's trunk to seal itself to the fuselage.

"I love the bustle of an airport." Mandy's voice was muffled as she pressed her nose to the window. Her eyes slid first one way, then the other as she craned to watch the ground crew prepare to move in and unload the luggage. The high pitched scream of the jet engines died down to a whimper as the pilot switched off.

"Come on, dreamer." She dragged her eyes from the outside scene at Susan's urging, and with a sigh of frustration sidled into the aisle, crouching as she moved from beneath the luggage rack.

"I think I'll be an airline pilot." Mandy dragged her flight bag from the rack. "Women are doing that kind of job these days, you know."

"Well, you'd better make up your mind." Susan led the way toward the exit, shuffling along slowly behind the other passengers. "Back to school in three days. Only one more year to go before university, and you still haven't a notion of what you really want to do in life."

"I have now." Mandy was quite sure. "I shall study in the field of aeronautical engineering."

"I'll believe it when I see it." Susan smiled. They moved along the ramp into the airport building. "During this holiday you've decided to be a missionary, a pediatrician, a geologist, and a fashion designer. That fails to include all the occupations you mentioned that were somehow associated with horses."

"That's quite all right," Mandy chuckled. "I'll be a flying children's doctor in deepest Africa, and wear my own specially designed clothes while prospecting for gold on weekends."

They reached the baggage claim area and, leaning themselves comfortably against a pillar, settled down to wait for their suitcases to appear on the endless conveyor that passed through the wall from the loading ramp.

"Who knows?" Susan wriggled her shoulders, scratching her back on the rough stonework. "Now that your father is a big lottery winner, you may be able to do all of those things."

"Yes! Wasn't that a surprise?" she exclaimed. "Who would have thought last night that I would be wakened by that telephone call this morning telling me that Dad had won a million?" She shook her head as if bewildered. "I still can hardly believe it."

"Your father will be back from Montreal this evening, with the cheque. I'm sure you'll believe it all right when you see it in writing." She grinned at her friend's excitement.

"A million dollars. Just think, a million dollars!"
With each word she jabbed her elbow in Susan's ribs.
"Sorry Sue, but it's so fantastic!" She swung round,
hugging her friend.

Susan rolled her eyes to the ceiling. "Now she's trying
to squeeze me to death." But her smile showed her
complaint was not serious. "Hey! There are our bags."
She pulled away from Mandy and almost ran to the
conveyor belt. Quickly she grasped two identical green
suitcases, and swung them from the conveyor belt to the
floor just before they disappeared through the gate in the
wall. She turned to see Mandy approaching, a big grin on
her face. "Now what are you grinning at?" She rubbed
her leg where she had bumped it with one of the cases.

"My imagination at work again," Mandy explained.
"I could picture you unable to lift both bags, and being
carried out on the conveyor with them, legs waving
wildly in the air."

Susan laughed with her as they picked up their bags
and moved toward the exit. Gradually they made their
way toward the doors, manoeuvering through the crowds
of passengers and waiting friends.

"Do you think that your father will keep his business
going?" Susan stepped on the rubber mat and the door
automatically swung open.

"I think so. He's been very successful in the interior
decorating business, and he really loves his work." The
girls came to a stop at the sidewalk edge. "Of course,"
Mandy continued, "perhaps he'll branch out into the
industrial market. Just imagine the scope there would be
in creating designs for aircraft decoration. Pink wings;
blue body; yellow tail; all covered with a glorious pattern
of spring flowers."

"Yuk!" Susan grimaced at the mental picture

conjured up by this description. "Perhaps you should become a missionary after all." Her eyes moved quickly along the row of vehicles parked at the curb. "Good old Toronto; just when you need a taxi, there's never one around."

"Excuse me, Miss." Susan started back, puzzled, as a man moved in front of her. He touched the peak of his cap. "Are you Miss Mandy Cain?"

"No, I'm Mandy Cain." Mandy moved beside Susan. She stared at the large sunglasses covering the upper part of the man's face.

"Your father arranged that I should meet you, and take you to the hotel."

"To the hotel?" Mandy was puzzled. "Why not to the house?"

"It's quite usual for a family to leave home for a few days in the present circumstances, Miss," he replied.

"What circumstances?"

"Like winning the lottery, silly," Susan said softly in her ear. "That way you avoid being annoyed, like having the press and television reporters knocking at your door all the time," she explained.

"But that would be exciting!" Mandy exclaimed. "I wouldn't want to miss that."

"Obviously your father does, so let's not hang around here any longer."

"This way, Miss." The man relieved Mandy of her suitcase, and walked a few yards to where a large, black limousine was parked. He opened the rear door. "Will you get in, please?" He moved in such a way as to block Susan from following her friend. "I'm very sorry, Miss, but I was instructed to pick up only Miss Cain."

"That's quite all right, driver. Susan can come with me." Mandy beckoned Susan to join her in the rear of the car.

The driver hesitated for a moment, then moving to one side he ushered her into the car, slamming the door closed almost before she was seated. Swiftly he threw their suitcases into the trunk, jumped into the driver's seat, and started the engine. The car started with a jerk, throwing the girls back into their seats. A puzzled frown creased Mandy's forehead as she studied the interior of the car. There was a glass partition behind the driver, and it and the windows were of a darkly tinted glass. She also noticed that there were no door or window handles. She was about to remark on this to Susan, when a row of bright lights flooded on above each of the windows. The effect was to turn the dark glass into mirrors; it was impossible to see outside, like trying to look out from a lighted room at night.

"Hey! What's going on?" Mandy leaned forward and banged on the dividing screen, but there was no response from the driver.

"Quickly! See if you have a piece of paper in your purse." Susan rummaged through her pocket. "Ha! I've got a pen." She waited impatiently while a bewildered Mandy searched for paper.

"I haven't got any paper, except these tissues."

"They'll do." Susan took one from her, and using her knee as a support, she drew a short line in the centre of the sheet. Then, glancing at her watch, she jotted down the time, 10:35. "Look," she said, motioning at the doors, "no handles, dark glass that we can't see through and a driver who ignores our questions."

"Kidnapped?" Mandy raised her eyebrows in question.

"Yes," she nodded. "Obviously somebody decided that you can provide them with a nice juicy ransom."

They swayed as the car turned a corner. Susan marked a small line protruding at right angles from the first line drawn on the tissue, again recording the time. Several times during the next six minutes they could feel the vehicle changing direction, and Susan faithfully recorded each move by drawing another little line and noting the time. They felt the car pick up speed as they obviously entered a major highway, the muffled roar of a large truck coming to their ears as they passed it.

"Why are you drawing a map?" Mandy asked as she cupped her hands around her eyes and pressed close to the windows. "You don't know whether we're heading north, south, east or west."

"I know, but if we can get a glimpse of the sun when we get out of the car, we should be able to work backwards along the map to see what direction we headed when we left the airport. Then, if we get a chance to smuggle the information out to your father or the police, they'll know where to look for us."

"Here, just a minute!" Mandy drew back from the window on her side, and scrambling inelegantly across Susan, pressed her face against the window of the other door. "Yes, look. If you cup your hands like this and look upwards, you'll notice that it's brighter on my side of the car. That must be south, where the sun is at this time of the day. No, say south-east."

"Good girl!" Susan placed an arrow on the tissue sloping diagonally across the last line that she had drawn, marking it with a letter N to signify north. They felt the car slowing and pulling slightly to the right; once more Susan noted the change of direction and recorded the time. The car stopped momentarily before turning right and accelerating again. Mandy moved from one window to the other, cupping her hands as she did so to shield her eyes from the harsh glare of the bright internal lights.

"We must be heading almost due north-west. Both windows seem to be the same, and the sun must be behind us now."

"I think we have just left Highway 401," Susan observed. "Did you notice that while we were bombing along, although we heard several trucks on the right side when we passed them, we heard no traffic passing in the other direction?"

"Why, of course!" Mandy agreed. "West of Toronto, the highway has a wide grass median between the east and westbound lanes; we wouldn't hear traffic travelling in the other direction."

During the next twelve and a half minutes, as noted by Susan, the car twisted and turned many times. Susan's map was beginning to look like a child's doodle, the lines crossing each other several times. Obviously the driver was taking a devious route to confuse them, or anybody who might be following. They heard the echo as the car passed under a bridge, a fact that was confirmed when they heard the heavy throb of a diesel engine and the faint clickety-clack of rail wheels. The car lurched from side to side as they turned off a smooth road onto a rough track. Periodically they could hear the scrape of undergrowth along the side of the car.

"Phew! What on earth is that horrible smell?" Mandy wrinkled her nose.

"Pigs."

"Who is?" Mandy looked at her belligerently.

"Nobody is. I meant, that's what you can smell. We must be close to a pig farm."

The car slowed and finally stopped. Susan quickly folded her tissue map and put it in her shoe; she slipped the pen up her sleeve.

"Grab some of those tissues from your purse, and put them in your shoes," she instructed Mandy, who hastened to comply. Just in time. They sat back in their seats as the door was opened. "Act scared," Susan whispered. "We might get a better chance to escape."

"Why have you brought us here?" Mandy quavered.

"And why are there no handles on the doors?" Susan shrank back as if in fear.

"Out." The driver motioned with his thumb but when Susan drew back even further, he reached in and grabbed her arm. Momentarily Susan resisted, clinging to the door frame with her free hand. Suddenly she allowed herself to be pulled out of the car, not into bright sunlight as they had expected, but into the gloom of what appeared to be an old barn. She snatched her arm free.

"Run for it!" She dodged sideways, evading the clutching hands of the driver, but Mandy was not so lucky. She was caught and firmly held. Susan rushed toward the barn door which had been closed after the car had entered, but another man, his face masked with a stocking, loomed out of the shadows and blocked her path. She looked around wildly, but it was clear that there was no other exit, and escape was impossible. Meekly she allowed herself to be half led and half pushed to join Mandy and her captor.

"That wasn't very clever, girlie," the driver sneered at her. "Any more tricks like that and I'll tie you up."

"What are you going to do with us?" Susan demanded.

"Whatever we decide to do with you, you won't like it, unless you behave yourselves. Come on!" He took both girls in a firm grip, pushing them toward a small door in the end wall. The other man opened the door, and they were pushed into a small, bare room. After their purses had been taken, the door was slammed. They heard the rattle of a chain, and the sound of a padlock being snapped shut. There was a burst of laughter as one of the men made a remark, the muffled click of receding footsteps, and then silence.

They stood just inside the door, their eyes darting from side to side as they examined their prison. The cell-like room was bare except for a pile of fresh straw in one corner. Mandy threw herself down on it. Now that the initial excitement was over, she began to feel perturbed.

"What do you think they will do with us?" A very slight trace of fear pitched her voice higher than normal.

"Keep us here as prisoners until they can collect ransom for you, I would imagine." Susan sounded far calmer and collected than she really felt. While she had had some exposure to danger during one or two criminal investigations, kidnapping was a new experience for her. She began to examine the small room carefully, seeking a possible escape route. Unfortunately the floor was of solid concrete and the walls of red brick. Apart from the door through which they had entered, there was no exit. The ceiling appeared to be made of plywood sheeting, but it was at least twelve feet above the floor and could not be reached. There was a small, glassless window frame close to the ceiling in one wall, which appeared to be far too small for either of them to pass through, even if they could find some way of reaching it. Moving backwards until she was pressing firmly against the door, Susan raised herself on her toes, straining to see out the window. Nothing. Nothing but a clear patch of blue sky; not even a single bird or a trace of cloud. She moved forward, the effect being the same as if she were standing next to the window, and swept her eyes upwards. Ha! That was interesting. She moved forward until she was almost touching the wall immediately below the window, and the patch of blue had narrowed to a mere slit in her line of vision. In that slit, however, she could just see the sagging web of high tension wires as they passed directly overhead. Moving sideways along the wall, first in one direction, then the other, she counted a total of eight strands; obviously a major power line. Having seen all there was to see, she dropped down on the straw beside Mandy, who was now staring sightlessly into space. Susan looked at her friend closely, noting the pale waxen skin, and a sheen of perspiration on her forehead and upper lip. She was displaying the classic symptoms of shock. The reaction to their unexpected abduction was setting in. It was time to give her something else to think about. Removing her own shoes, Susan retrieved the map.

"Let me have a clean tissue, would you please, Mandy?"

"Eh? What?" Mandy looked bewildered.

"I need a clean tissue," Susan explained patiently.

"A clean tissue?" she repeated. Then understanding came back to her eyes. "Oh, a clean tissue. Just a minute." She also slipped off her shoes, and retrieved the three or four folded sheets. "Here you are."

Susan brushed an area of the floor clear of straw, and smoothed out one of the tissues.

"I want to try calculating how far we are from the airport, and in which direction. Then . . ." She broke off as the sound of a low flying jet aircraft filled the room, drowning the sound of her voice. As quickly as it had come, the plane droned off into the distance.

"We must be pretty close to the airport at Malton if

airplanes fly over here so low," Mandy observed.

"Certainly no more than four or five miles, I would say." Susan knitted her brows. "If I remember correctly, the main runways at Toronto run north-east to south-west, and north-west to south-east. With the wind blowing from the north-east, as it is today, aircraft would land from the south-west."

"I didn't notice any wind blowing at all. What makes you so positive that there is a wind, and that it's blowing from the direction you say it is?"

"Don't you remember? Just before we arrived at Toronto the pilot told us that the temperature was eighty degrees Fahrenheit, the sky was clear, and the wind was from the north-east at ten miles per hour?" Susan asked.

"I guess that's why I'll never make a detective like you," Mandy sighed. "I always forget to remember."

"Never mind," Susan smiled. "Let's see if we can redraw the map to scale, and work out how far we travelled in the car." Mandy looked much better. Colour had returned to her cheeks and her eyes had regained most of their usual sparkle.

"Mark this off in finger widths; then you can use it as a ruler." Mandy selected a thick, straight straw.

"That's a good idea." Susan marked the straw with her pen as Mandy held it flat to the floor. "Let's assume that for the first part of the trip we averaged thirty miles an hour."

"From the airport to where we turned onto the highway?"

"Right. Then let's say we moved at sixty on the highway, dropping to, say twenty, as an average, from the highway to this farm."

Mandy wrinkled her brow in concentration as she

mentally calculated. "That means we travelled a half mile in one minute, one mile a minute, and one third of a mile per minute respectively, for each section."

"Very good," Susan grinned. "I'll put a gold star in your book."

"So if we convert those distances to finger widths," (Mandy ignored Susan's interruption) "allowing one width to equal one third of a mile, then for each of the three parts of the trip you'll get, er . . ." She looked to Susan for help.

"One and a half finger widths per minute at thirty miles an hour, three widths per minute at sixty, and one per minute at twenty."

"Just what I was going to say." Mandy wrinkled her nose at her friend's smile of amusement. "Well, perhaps not as quickly," she admitted.

"Okay then, let's get to it." Susan placed a dot in the centre of the sheet to represent the barn. "You call off the direction and the number of finger widths between each turn, working backwards, and I'll draw the new map."

They worked industriously for several minutes, occasionally pausing to discuss and resolve a point of doubt. Fortunately the majority of rural roads to the west of Toronto are laid out in a grid, and all turns are therefore ninety degrees. This greatly simplified their task and quite soon Susan sank back on her heels.

"Well! Look at that." She raised her eyebrows in surprise.

"Why, we must have travelled thirty miles or so, yet we seem to be almost exactly eight miles from the airport." Mandy measured the straight line distance between the starting and ending points. "Look how the driver doubled back on himself several times."

Just then the scream of another aircraft came to their ears. Susan jumped up and quickly moved to peer upwards and outwards through the window. She was just in time to see an orange jumbo jet flash across the opening, so low that it looked as if it would scrape the hydro wires. As soon as she could make herself heard, Susan rejoined Mandy.

"That settles it. I'm sure that we are no more than five or six miles from the end of the main north-east to south-west runway at Malton." She noted the distance on the map. She also measured the distance from the highway, which could only be Highway 401; about two miles, considering that the bridge they had passed under was halfway between the highway and the barn.

The door chain rattled. "Quickly, cover the map!" The girls spread loose straw over the tissue.

"Here's your lunch." The man in the stocking mask entered, carrying a wooden tray on which there was a paper plate holding some sandwiches and two cans of cola.

"Why are you keeping us here? Let us out!" the girls demanded in unison, beginning to climb to their feet. Quickly the man placed the tray on the floor just inside the door, and backed out without answering their questions.

"At least it looks as if they don't want us to starve," Susan observed as she rose to pick up the food.

Slowly the afternoon dragged by and the bright rectangle of light thrown on the opposite wall by the sun streaming through the window slowly moved along and up. Several times Susan tried flashing a mirror at a landing aircraft, but on each occasion it passed the opening so quickly that it was doubtful if the pilot would have seen the brief flash. They also tried removing a brick in one of the walls, but with no metal instruments it was obvious that the task was virtually impossible.

It was almost dark when once again they heard the rattle of the padlock being removed. Susan readied herself to make a dash for it, but she sank back when she saw that both men were standing at the door. Wordlessly, the man in the stocking mask beckoned Susan to bring the tray to him. She complied, receiving another tray holding two boxes of fried chicken in return. The other man, the driver, rolled two cans of cola across the floor to Mandy. Stocking Face backed out of the room, returning immediately with two rugs which he dropped on the floor just inside the door. Without having uttered a word, the captors slammed the door, and the girls heard the padlock being replaced.

"It looks as if we shall be here for quite a while — certainly until sometime tomorrow, I should think." Susan picked up the tray and eased herself down next to Mandy.

"If only he hadn't won the lottery, this never would have happened! If only the newspapers hadn't publicized his win, these men would not have thought of kidnapping."

"Iffing isn't going to help." Susan put her mind seriously to thoughts of escape or rescue. Apart from scratching away at the cement binding the bricks in the wall, and flashing a mirror at passing aircraft, they had accomplished nothing. Mentally she added their assets: one ball-point pen, two clean tissues, a mirror — now back in Mandy's pocket — two empty cola cans, and two full ones. Up to this point a number of vague thoughts had floated through Susan's mind, but now it was time to marshal them into some kind of order. Her eyes wandered around the small room, examining walls, floor and ceiling for possible weaknesses. Perhaps they could use the mirror to reflect the sun and start a fire in the straw! She shook her head as she discarded the thought. They would require some means of focusing the sun's rays, something like a magnifying glass, and that they did not have. After several minutes of hard thinking while she ate her chicken, Susan reluctantly concluded that escape was not possible from the room. If they had an opportunity to get out into the barn proper, there might be a chance, but the men were being very careful. She looked across at Mandy who was sitting staring into space once more.

"Mandy, we must be ready to send some kind of message to your father or the police."

"How on earth can we send messages?" Her voice held an impatient note. She was getting very anxious and depressed as she thought of her parents worrying over her absence.

"Sooner or later the kidnappers will get in touch with your father to demand ransom, if they haven't already done so. Perhaps we could persuade them to let you write a note to him, and we could include a coded message to tell him where we are."

"That's no good; he wouldn't expect a coded letter." Mandy put her thoughts to the matter. After two or three seconds her face lightened. "If we could manage to include your tissue map with the letter, he'd know exactly where to find us!"

"Yes, I suppose you're right." Mandy slumped down into the straw, sitting up again almost immediately as a fresh thought crossed her mind. "Your uncle is a policeman. If *you* wrote a letter in code, he might spot it."

"Now there's a thought!" Susan pondered the

suggestion. "I'll ask if I may send one to my father. He's bound to show it to Uncle Ted."

Now it was quite dark, the small rectangle of the window framing a cluster of stars in the moonless sky. Periodically one of the girls climbed to her feet and walked about in the confined area to relieve the enforced idleness. They had played numerous word games using the remaining tissues and the empty fried chicken boxes until it had become too dark to continue. For a while they shouted as loudly as possible, in case somebody was within hearing distance, but with no noticeable results other than sore throats. Susan then lay back on the straw, covering herself with one of the rugs when the temperature fell, mentally composing the letter she intended to write if given the opportunity.

The silence was broken abruptly as the padlock was removed and the door swung open. The beam of a flashlight sprang across the room, causing the girls to squint. It took several seconds before their eyes were well enough adjusted to recognize Stocking Face. He beckoned to Mandy to return the tray. As she reached him, he grabbed her arm, pulled her from the room and slammed the door.

"Hey!" Susan jumped to her feet, and ran to the door, pounding on it with her fists. "Where are you taking her?" she shouted, but there was no reply. She threw herself at the door, but soon gave it up as a useless exercise. Puzzled, she returned to the pile of straw, and, wrapping the rugs about her shoulders, sat down to wait. Five minutes later the door opened once more, and Mandy was thrust back into the room.

"It's all right," Mandy assured her. "He's only going to take you to a washroom so that you can clean up. Look, he even let me bring my transistor radio. Now the time should pass faster."

"That's a relief." Susan climbed to her feet in response to a waved instruction from Stocking Face. "In more ways than one!" She allowed herself to be escorted out into the night, and across to the looming mass of a nearby house. She took the opportunity to look about, but in the moonless night she could discern no details of the house or the surrounding countryside. Looking backwards over her shoulder, however, she observed that the night sky was much brighter in the direction where she supposed Toronto to be. Peering upwards, she could just make out that high tension wires did, indeed, pass directly overhead; they were just visible against the stars.

"It's very frightening being shut up in that old barn without a light. Couldn't we have a flashlight or something?"

Stocking Face merely grunted in reply as he led her along a passage into an unlit room in the house. He thrust her inside; then, before she could follow, he quickly withdrew and slammed the door. Almost immediately a single, naked light bulb came on above the door. She looked around the small room, shading her eyes against the harsh light. Apart from a small cracked sink and a toilet, the room was bare, and had that air of a neglected house. She felt sure that no woman lived in the house, and that perhaps either or both of the men were bachelors. Reaching this conclusion brought a certain amount of relief. It could provide the answer to a question that had troubled her all afternoon. Stocking Face had concealed his identity from the very first, perhaps because he was known to Mandy. The driver had taken no such precautions, either because he knew that the girls would be in no position to identify him later, or because he intended to leave the country. The deserted appearance indicated that the house was not a permanent home, and that the men intended to leave as soon as a ransom had been paid. There was a single window, but it was boarded up from the outside and Susan could see that even if she smashed the glass she would not be able to dislodge the shutter. Almost before she had finished drying her hands on a scrap of toweling hung on a nail behind the door, the light went out. She stepped back as the door opened, and again was dazzled as the flashlight was aimed directly at her face.

"Here." A hand came into the lightbeam, holding a lamp. Gratefully Susan took it, and allowed herself to be marched back to the barn to rejoin Mandy. Before closing and locking the door, the man struck a match and lit the lamp. He left with a gruff caution: "Don't expect anybody to come and save you if you set fire to that straw." The chain rattled, and his footsteps faded away.

"Oh, that's good," Mandy exclaimed in relief. "It's not that I'm frightened of the dark exactly, but I wasn't looking forward to spending the night here with no light at all."

"Do you recognize anything familiar about that man?" Susan asked as the girls settled themselves in the straw, drawing together for comfort, the rugs pulled snugly about their shoulders.

"I don't think so." She shook her head.

"I'm quite sure you'd recognize him without that mask."

"Perhaps you're right. I certainly prefer him to that creepy driver."

Susan switched on the radio, tuning in first a Toronto station, and then one from Hamilton, a neighbouring city. The first was quite loud, and the second much less audible. She twisted the radio and the volume swelled.

She moved it backwards and forwards, the music rising and falling until, at last, Mandy complained.

"For goodness sake, stop playing with it! Put it down."

"Just a minute." A vague memory was stirring at the back of Susan's mind. Something to do with radio direction finding. "Got it!" Her outburst brought another muttered complaint from Mandy, who was very close to sleep. "Wake up. I remember reading somewhere that a radio signal is strongest when the antenna is in line with a transmitter. So, if I turn the radio until the volume is at its loudest, the built-in antenna that runs along the inside of the case must be in line with the station. There!" She placed the transistor on the cement floor at the edge of the straw.

By this time Mandy was wide awake once more, and she offered her contribution. "We know that the window faces west; therefore, the signal must be coming from the south-east or the north-west. It just helps to confirm our map."

"That's right, and because we know that we are north of Hamilton, Toronto must be south-east of here. It can't be north-west," Susan concluded.

"If we could locate a few other Ontario cities, such as Paris or Kitchener, we should be able to pinpoint exactly where we are."

Susan tuned in to other stations, but, probably because of the interference of the high-tension wires overhead, she could not clearly identify them.

"Oh well, let's forget it and get some sleep." Mandy turned on her side, burrowing deeper into the straw as she made herself comfortable.

It could hardly be described as a good night by either of the girls; it seemed endless. At last they noticed a lightening at the window. A little later their jailers brought them breakfast, consisting of a selection of doughnuts and paper cups of coffee. While not too appetizing, it was at least nourishing, and stopped the rumbles in their stomachs. Their spirits rose as the day became brighter. They discussed their captors; Susan was now quite convinced that the girls would not come to any physical harm. Why else would they be fed, given blankets for warmth, and the lamp for comfort? Mandy felt that she now found Stocking Face familiar, but she couldn't put a name to him, or even a place or a time when she may have met him. Susan put forward a number of suggestions — perhaps he worked for Mandy's father, or perhaps he was a neighbour or a family friend — but none helped solidify Mandy's ideas.

Just after ten o'clock the men returned, the driver carrying a writing pad, envelopes, and a pencil. He thrust them at Mandy.

"Here. Write to your father. Tell him that you are well, and that he must do as we instruct."

"Could I write to *my* father?" Susan asked. "Please?" she added plaintively.

"No!" He grunted the one word answer.

"Aw, let her write." Stocking Face stood just outside the door. "It'll help put the pressure on Cain to pay up."

The first man hesitated; then, reluctantly nodding his agreement, he took another pencil stub from his pocket and threw it in Susan's direction. It fell into the straw, and while she was searching for it Susan took the opportunity to slip the tissue map into her palm. She had been thinking of what she should say since first waking up, and now she quickly scribbled a few lines. Moving her body so that she could conceal her movements, she folded the note, enclosing the tissue map so that it was not visible. Lastly she wrote her father's name and address on the outside. She waited for Mandy to fold her note; then, taking it from her, she passed both to the driver, Mandy's uppermost.

"Just a moment!" Stocking Face held out his hand for the notes. He unfolded Susan's, and the map fluttered to the floor. He picked it up and looked at it. Then, without saying a word, he crumpled it and thrust it in his pocket.

"What's that!" the other man demanded.

"Just a stupid map the girls drew."

"Oh, is that right?" He turned menacingly toward them. "Any more tricks like that and you'll be sorry," he threatened. He almost pushed Stocking Face from the room, and they could hear him complaining in a loud voice as the padlock was secured.

"I agree." Mandy sat back, propped up by her elbows. "Every time I see the man in the stocking, I become more convinced that there is something very familiar about him. He's certainly a much nicer man than the other. But I wish he hadn't spotted your map."

"Never mind. It was worth the try." Susan seemed very cheerful as she turned on the radio and hummed along with the music.

The day dragged by, uninterrupted except on two occasions when the girls were led across to the house to freshen up. Each time they were taken individually, and they were blindfolded. Mandy reported that she had clearly heard a train passing on the line which they had estimated to be about a mile south. Susan could hear nothing on her visits other than a subdued, but fairly constant, humming sound, which she felt sure was the noise of traffic on the freeway some miles away. During the night the weather had changed considerably. It was now overcast, and frequent rain squalls sent showers of water through the glassless window. They moved the straw to remain dry, covering themselves with the rugs for protection from the odd drop, carried by the swirling gusts, which fell on them. The wind had shifted, blowing from the north, and no aircraft passed over on its way to the airport.

"Do you think there is any chance of being released today?" Mandy broke one of the long silences.

"No, I don't think so." Susan shook her head. "I think that the men will probably send our letters and their demands by mail, and they won't be delivered until tomorrow morning. It's my guess that nothing will happen until tomorrow afternoon at the earliest."

"I'll go mad with boredom, just sitting, staring at these four walls. Can't we do something?" Mandy implored.

Susan sat up and leaned her back against the wall, staring up at the window thoughtfully. Mentally she measured the size of the aperture; then she looked down at her friend.

"You're thinner than I am. If you climbed up on my shoulders, do you think you could get your shoulders through the window?"

Mandy followed her gaze, and then met her eyes with disbelief. "I might be thin, but not as skinny as that! Why, that window's no wider than a foot," she protested.

"I know; but it's about nine inches high, and therefore it must be something like fifteen inches from corner to corner," Susan explained.

"Well, all right," Mandy said, climbing to her feet. "I'm game if you are."

Susan stood directly beneath the window, facing the

wall. She crouched down, arms stretched forward with her hands flat against the bricks. Mandy gingerly stepped up on Susan's thigh, and then, steadying herself with a hand on the wall, climbed until she stood on her friend's shoulders. Susan tried to rise, straining with the effort.

"It's no good," she panted. "We'll have to try something different." Mandy jumped to the floor, and Susan straightened, ruefully rubbing her shoulders. "Would you mind removing your shoes next time?"

"Sorry, Sue." She kicked off her shoes.

"Look," Susan instructed after a moment's thought. "I'll bend forward from the waist, but I'll keep my legs straight. You climb up and stand on the small of my back; then, as I straighten up, step onto my shoulders."

This time their efforts were successful, and shortly Mandy was standing with the top edge of the window level with her chin. She crouched slightly, and poked her head through the frame. Quickly she looked around, but neither of the men was in sight. Twisting her shoulders, she pushed them through the narrow opening. Susan felt the weight lighten and, lifting her hands, she slipped them under Mandy's feet. Mandy wriggled as Susan pushed upwards. Briefly it seemed as if Mandy was about to slip out easily but then she stuck, her arms pinned firmly to her sides.

"Get me down!" she hissed loudly to Susan. But no matter how hard Susan pulled, Mandy did not budge. Her weight was acting against her now, making it impossible for her to move in or out. They tried for several minutes until, at last, quite breathless, Susan told her to call for help. To Mandy, shoulders becoming more bruised by the minute, hair and face drenched by rain, it seemed like hours before her shouts were at last rewarded by the appearance of the driver. Mandy had found to her great surprise that the ground outside the room was just below the window as though the end of the barn had been built into a hill. The driver had climbed the slope and his shoes were a few inches below Mandy's face as he towered over her. Looking at his feet and then up to his face she feared what he might do next. She closed her eyes in dread anticipation, but when nothing happened she opened them again to find that he had walked away.

"Hey!" she called, fear forgotten. "You can't leave me here like this." She started to wriggle again, but soon became short of breath. Suddenly she was grabbed around the waist from behind, and dragged roughly backwards through the frame, skinning her upper arms.

"I warned you!" He stepped down the short ladder, carrying Mandy like a sack of potatoes under his arm. He dropped her onto her hands and knees, and she scurried away from him. Picking up the ladder, he started for the door. "One more piece of nonsense, and I'll tie both of you so that you can't move." It was obvious that he was in deadly earnest. Neither of the girls dared say a word, and they sat as quiet as mice until he had left the room, padlocking the door as he went.

"Fine idea that was!" Mandy snorted when they were again alone.

"Well, it nearly worked," Susan offered lamely. "If you had put your arms through first, instead of your head, I'm sure you would be free now."

"Look at my arms!" Mandy wailed. "All that good suntan, gone!"

The long day finally drew to a close. Perhaps in ·punishment for their escape bid, the captives were brought no supper. Despite their empty stomachs, they slept much more soundly than they had the previous night, and it was soon dawn. The morning passed, but still no food appeared. Just before noon, when they were sure they were about to die of thirst, the girls suddenly heard the clatter of a helicopter. Quickly Susan jumped to her feet, and craned her head to see out the window. She raised her hand to shade her eyes from the sun, which was again shining brightly from a cloudless sky.

"Where's your mirror?" She held out her hand, snapping her fingers impatiently as Mandy feverishly searched her pockets. "Never mind." She scrabbled in the straw and picked up the radio. While polishing the chrome trim of the transistor on her sleeve, she moved toward the window. She looked up, squinting against the sun. Just then, as she had hoped, the helicopter floated into view. Holding the radio in the sunlight, Susan rocked it backwards and forwards, the chrome reflecting the beam like a mirror. The note of the helicopter engine deepened, and slowly the machine began to descend, moving out of her sight. The engine noise faded completely, and they stood waiting uncertainly, not sure that their signal had been seen. Five minutes passed. Six. Seven. Susan slumped to the straw. Suddenly they could hear muffled shouting. A car engine started, raced for a second, and then stopped again. The girls jumped up and ran to the door. Together they banged on it with their fists.

"Here we are! Here we are, in the barn!" they shouted in unison. The chain rattled, and they backed away from the door, half fearful. It opened slowly.

"Don't just stand there. Don't you want to go home?" Susan's Uncle Ted was smiling broadly as he held out his arms to them.

"So that's who it was!" Mandy sat wrapped in her dressing gown, warm and relaxed after a long refreshing soak in the bath. "He's such a nice man. How did he ever become involved with that horrible driver?''

"An all too familiar story, I'm afraid, my dear," her father began. "He became such a compulsive gambler that he preferred to spend his time at the race track, and I was forced to discharge him just over a year ago. After that he just got deeper and deeper in debt, and was easy prey when the other man suggested kidnapping you for ransom."

"But he isn't all bad, is he?" Mandy suggested. "After all, he was coming to tell you when you met him leaving the farm."

"Yes, I'm quite convinced that he was. I'm sure that he found the other man's behaviour toward you children quite upsetting; he was always a gentle person."

They sat in silence for a few minutes, each busy with his or her thoughts. Mandy's father and mother sat on each side of their daughter, pleased and relieved to have her back safe and sound. Susan lay in one of her comfortable positions on the floor, flat on her back, head cradled in her hands. Her father and her policeman uncle lolled comfortably in their chairs facing her.

"Just a minute." Mandy broke the silence. Her voice was puzzled. "If you caught him at the entrance to the farm, that means that you were already on the way to rescue us. How did you know where to look?"

"We saw the mirror flashing through the barn window." Mr. Cain pretended not to understand her question, a smile tugging at his lips as he teased her.

"You know what I mean," Mandy insisted. "How did you know that we were at that particular spot? We could have been almost anywhere in the country."

"Susan told us in her letter," Uncle Ted answered.

"But I saw that awful driver read Susan's letter, and I'm sure he would not have mailed it if she had written details of where we were being held."

"It was in code," Susan explained. "Remember? You suggested it."

"May I see it, please?" Mandy turned to Uncle Ted. She took the letter from him and read it aloud.

Dear Dad,

First let's say we are well treated. When we arrived here at the beginning, personally I got frightened and really miserable. I'm now behaving and reacting normally, much less tense now, slowly vanishing nervousness, maybe I'll laugh eventually, eh? Make certain that we're out soon; certainly not overjoyed now evening's starting to hasten. How are my two nieces? Still well? Have you decided regarding our overseas holidays, Dad? The weather on Majorca entices naturally, not only good natural sunshine, some exciting eventful nightlife. Endless attractions; let's go there, shall we? I realize this is hardly the time to talk of holidays, but it helps take my mind away from this situation. Looking forward to being home again soon. Give my love to Uncle Ted and his girls.

Love,
Susan

She read it to herself once more before turning to Susan. "I didn't know that you were thinking of going to Majorca next year." Then she turned to Susan's Uncle Ted. "What girls does she mean? You don't have any daughters. Apart from those things, and Susan's usual murder of the English language, I see nothing odd about the letter. Certainly no information telling you where to find us.''

"Here, let me show you." Uncle Ted held out his hand for the letter. He took a pen from his pocket to serve as a pointer. "The first clue was when she asked her father to pass on her love to me. He reasoned that she wanted me to see the letter. Now, as I am a policeman, my naturally inquisitive mind suggested that there must be more to the letter than appears on the surface. As soon as I saw the first two words, I knew it was in code.''

'' 'First let's?' '' Mandy read over his shoulder. "What does that tell you?''

"If you say it slowly, emphasizing the syllables, you might see it. Listen: 'First — let — sss.' Doesn't that sound like, 'First letters'?'' Mandy nodded. "Right, then. Now, in the next sentence you see the word 'beginning', and about three sentences from the end of the letter you see the word 'Endless'.'' Again Mandy nodded her head. "So, now if I write down the first letters of all the words between 'beginning' and 'endless', this is what I get.''

He jotted down the letters at the foot of the sheet of paper, placing the punctuation marks as they were spaced in the letter. PIGFARM. INBARN, MLTN, SVN, MILE, E?MCTWOS; CNONESTH. HAMTN, SW?HYDROOH, D? TWOMEN, NOGNS, SEEN.

"I see it!" Mandy burst out gleefully. "Let me read it out. 'Pig farm, in barn, Malton Airport, seven miles east. MacDonald Cartier Freeway, two south. Canadian National one south. Hamilton, south-west. Hydro-lines overhead. Two men, no guns seen.' '' She looked at her friend with admiration. "Oh, you smart kid!" Then she frowned in pretended annoyance. "And all the time you let me think that you were relying on the tissue map, and that they had foiled us when they discovered it.'' She slipped from her chair to her knees beside her friend. ''I thought it was fishy, the way you were so unconcerned when they found the map, but I didn't suspect a red herring.''

They all burst into laughter followed by the usual groans that greet a good pun.

Susan Super Sleuth and The Crime at Coulter Cove

ue! Sue! Over here, Sue!''
She jumped up and down, waving her hand above her head, straining to see over the crowd that swirled about in front of her on the platform.

Susan heard the shrill voice over the babble of conversations and the deep throb of the diesel locomotive. Her face split into a wide grin as she spotted her friend. She waved vigorously in reply.

"Coming, Kathy.'' She picked as her guide the top of a towering fir tree which stood just behind Kathy before stepping down among the crowd of happy holiday-makers. A large suitcase in one hand, a tennis racket in the other, a small knapsack swinging from one shoulder, and a camera slung round her neck, Susan edged forward through the crowd. Struggling to hold on to all her belongings, she kept her eye on the tree top as she wriggled forward. Finally, with a most unladylike shoulder charge which brought a disapproving frown from a very prim old lady blocking her way, Susan burst free, almost tripping over her suitcase in her efforts.

"Whoops! I've got you." The kindly faced, white haired gentleman standing with Kathy caught Susan's arm, just in time to stop her from crashing to the ground.

"Thanks." With a sigh of relief, Susan dropped the case, clenching and unclenching her fingers to restore the circulation. She looked at her cousin as she brushed the hair from her eyes with a careless sweep of the tennis racket. "Whew! After that battle, I feel as if I've earned a holiday." Then, without stopping for breath, she continued, "How are you, Kathy? It seems simply ages since I last saw you."

"All of five weeks," Kathy laughed in reply. She had stopped off briefly at Toronto on her way from Truro, Nova Scotia, at the beginning of the vacation.

"May not seem long to you," Susan snorted. "I'm the one that had to stay in sweltering old Toronto going to summer school."

"Serves you right." Kathy turned to her uncle with a smile. "She spends all of her time reading detective books, then wonders why she fails her subjects." Then, raising a quizzical eyebrow, she said, "Oh, I'm sorry, Uncle Jim; you haven't met Susan before, have you?" She threw her arm around Susan's shoulders. "Uncle Jim, this is Susan, my favourite cousin, and my best friend. Susan, this is my Uncle Jim."

"How are you, Susan?" He put out his hand. "I've heard a lot about you."

"Oh dear!" Susan pulled down the corners of her lips in pretended alarm, opening her eyes wide, eyebrows climbing. "Perhaps I'd better get right back onto the train."

"No, no. Nothing bad, I assure you." He chuckled.

"In that case —" she grasped his hand in both of hers and vigorously pumped it up and down — "I'm very pleased to meet you, Mister, er . . ."

"Mister Tisdale, if you insist, but I'd much rather you call me Jim." Then, at the slight trace of embarrassment that slipped across her face, "Or, *Uncle* Jim, if you'd prefer."

"Yes, that's better. Uncle Jim. I'll adopt you as my uncle while I'm here."

"Right. That's settled then. Come on, you two; I'm starving." Kathy picked up the suitcase, the sudden effort causing her to gasp. "What have you got in this case? A ton of cement?" She staggered off towards the parking lot. Her uncle caught up with her, and, relieving her of the load, led the chattering girls to the car. In a very few minutes they were on their way.

"Look at those mountains." Susan leaned forward to peer upwards through the windshield at the soaring peaks which towered above them. The car moved smoothly and swiftly along the road, a broad, merrily bubbling stream on their left, and mountains climbing to the cloudless blue skies on both sides of the valley. Gradually the valley widened; then, swinging round a steep bluff, the road suddenly burst into a huge sweeping bowl. A beautiful wide lake shimmered in the sunlight and spread out like a huge blue mirror, reflecting the distant, snow-capped peaks. A number of small boats, white sails billowing lazily in the breeze, glided across the water.

"Oh! Isn't it wonderful." Susan gazed about her, face beaming. She turned in her seat to look accusingly at Kathy, who was watching her reaction with obvious delight. "Why didn't you tell me it was like this?"

"I did, several times." Kathy grinned.

"Well, you should have tried harder to make me

understand. If I had known, I would have worked harder. Just think," her voice rose, "I've been knocking my brains out at summer school, while all the time you've been lazing around in this heaven." She snorted, turning to face forward again, just in time to catch a glimpse of a sign as they entered the small village: *Coulter Cove — Population 310.*

"Only three hundred and ten people?" Susan voiced her surprise.

"Ah, that's only the number of permanent residents. Right now, there are more like three times that number." Uncle Jim pointed up to the tree-lined slopes climbing above the village main street. "Up there, if you look closely, you'll see many summer cottages hidden among the trees. That's where most of our seasonal visitors live."

They ran through the village. Then, slowing the car, Uncle Jim turned off the road onto a wide driveway that swept in a graceful curve to the entrance of a large hotel. Built of what appeared to be rough-hewn logs and dark red bricks, it soared five stories high. Despite its imposing height, it was so cleverly designed that it blended smoothly with the wooded slopes rising behind, not at all ugly or out of step with its surroundings.

"Doesn't it look just like a huge Swiss chalet?" Kathy hung over the back of the front seat, her head between those of Susan and her uncle.

"Yes, the steep, peaked roof and wooden beams look just like the picture postcards from Switzerland." Susan studied the building, her eyes sweeping across the rows of sparkling windows, and down to the imposing, canopied main entrance.

"What's this?" She peered into the dense shadow at the vehicle parked directly in front of the door. "Isn't that a police car?''

"Oh dear! Not again,'' Uncle Jim sighed.

"What is it?'' Susan turned in some alarm at the sad tone of his voice.

"There have been a number of thefts from the guest rooms lately,'' Kathy answered. "It looks as if there may have been another.''

Uncle Jim pulled in behind the police car, and, without waiting for the girls, hurried into the hotel lobby.

"Now, tell me all about it.'' Susan hung up her last pair of jeans, and slamming the lid of the now empty suitcase, she slipped it on the shelf of the closet. The girls were in their room on the third floor, at the front of the building. For several weeks Kathy had enjoyed the room to herself, but she was pleased that at long last Susan had arrived, even though this meant sharing a room. Uncle Jim was very nice, and he had made sure that she always had plenty to do, such as horseback riding, swimming, sailing, and tennis. But after a while these activities became boring without someone to share them with. Now that Susan had arrived there would be many more things to do together. They met quite infrequently, perhaps only once each year, but when they did meet something exciting happened. Much as she loved her life in Truro, it always seemed dull compared to Susan's.

"Come on then,'' Susan urged. "When did these mysterious thefts first start?'' She threw herself face downwards on her bed, propping her chin in her hands so that she could look directly at Kathy who sat on her own bed, comfortably leaning back against two doubled-up pillows.

"I knew that you would want to know exactly what had happened, so I jotted everything down that I could think of." Kathy leaned over and took a small notebook from the drawer in the bedside table. She thumbed through the pages. "Here we are. The first theft was about four weeks before I arrived, but since then we've had five more. Poor old Uncle Jim; it really is upsetting for him, although he tries hard not to show it. He's managed this hotel since long before I was born, and this is the first time that anything like this has happened to him."

"That was a Mountie car, wasn't it?" Susan asked. Then, in response to her own question, she continued, "Of course. Only Ontario and Quebec have their own provincial police forces; out here the Mounties police the smaller towns and villages." Having settled that point in her mind, she returned to the topic. "Have the police questioned the staff? Do they have any leads? What days of the week were the robberies? What kinds of things were taken? Wha . . .?"

"Whoa! Wait a minute." Kathy laughed, holding up her hand to stop the flow. She knew her cousin of old, always ready to jump in and play detective. "Come on, we'll go downstairs and see if Uncle Jim wants to talk about it." She wriggled off the bed and headed for the door, closely followed by an eager Susan. She led the way along the carpeted corridor toward the elevator.

"Oh no, you don't!" Susan grasped her arm firmly and steered her toward the stairs. "It'll take ages for the elevator to come, and besides, the exercise will be good for you."

"I might have known that my holiday would be over once you arrived." Kathy sighed in pretended sorrow, but her sparkling eyes belied her words. As always, Susan made her feel vibrantly alive, every minute promising excitement and adventure. She even made horrible chores like tidying up a bedroom occasions for joking and laughter.

"At least you'll be in shape when we go home," Susan called over her shoulder as she set off headlong down the stairs, closely followed by Kathy.

They burst into the high-ceilinged lobby with its bright red carpet. Kathy led the way to the manager's office, which was tucked away behind the reception desk. She tapped on the door; it was unlatched, and opened under her touch. They started to move forward into the room, only to stop quickly when they saw that Uncle Jim was not alone.

"No, don't go, girls. Come on in." He beckoned them forward. "Corporal Davis, this is my niece, Kathy — you may have met her before — and this is my newly-adopted niece, Susan." He nodded at each in turn as he said their names. "Susan and Kathy, I'd like you to meet Corporal Davis."

"Hi, girls." The corners of his eyes crinkled as he rose smiling, holding out his hand to them in turn. After a few pleasantries he retrieved his hat from the top of the filing cabinet that stood in the corner of the little room. "I'll be on my way then, Jim, but I'll be back with the sergeant tomorrow. Don't worry; we'll get to the bottom of this little problem." With a wave of his hand he left the office, pulling the door closed. Kathy sprang to her feet, and pushed the door to make sure it was latched.

" 'Get to the bottom of this little problem,' eh?" she exploded. "There have been numerous thefts, and they're no closer to finding the thief than they were before the first one happened!"

"Now, now, Kathy, it isn't easy, you know." Uncle Jim tried to pacify her, gently moving his hands up and down in front of his chest as he motioned her to sit down.

"The corporal and the sergeant are doing their best, but they have a large territory to cover."

"I bet Susan could do better!" Kathy threw out the challenge.

"Oh yes, Kathy has told me of your success in crime solving." He smiled at Susan. "Shall I ask the sergeant if you may sit in tomorrow?"

"Heck, I've just been lucky." Susan scuffed the carpet with her toe, embarrassed. But Uncle Jim wasn't fooled. He had noticed the gleam that came into her eyes as he had voiced his suggestion.He chuckled as he stood up and stretched. "Perhaps it's time for you to be lucky again. I'm sure you'll think so after dinner. Let's go." He ushered them out of his office and across the lobby to the dining room.

They spent a short but happy evening moving around the hotel, meeting many of the guests. For a brief period they managed to persuade Uncle Jim to join them in a game of scrabble, but it was still quite early when Susan could no longer suppress her yawns. She immediately agreed when Uncle Jim suggested that she must be very tired after her long journey, and would be better off in bed. Already she felt quite at home in the hotel, as if she had lived there for weeks instead of just a few hours. Was it only that morning that she had waved goodbye to her parents at the station in Toronto?

Uncle Jim's office was far too small for all of them to sit in comfort when they gathered the next morning, so at his suggestion they moved to the deserted lobby. Seated comfortably around a low coffee table, Susan and Kathy listened intently as Sergeant Fenton outlined the sequence of thefts, and the steps taken in their investigations so far.

"Now girls, is there anything else that you would like

to know?'' the sergeant asked, his quick wink at Corporal Davis not going unnoticed by Susan. Obviously he was prepared to answer their questions, but it was equally evident that he was not going to take them seriously. Up to this point she had been interested in learning the facts, more with the view of offering suggestions to Uncle Jim to prevent future crimes, rather than actively becoming involved in the affair. But that wink! Very well, she'd show this skeptical policeman that they weren't just silly little girls to be pacified because they were in some way related to the hotel manager.

"Never mind, sergeant. Thank you, but I am sure that you are busy enough without answering my stupid questions.'' She wanted to get away so she could start her own investigations. She would solve this case! And without the help of the local Mounted Police contingent. Well! Would you believe it? She compressed her lips in anger as she caught him winking again, this time at Uncle Jim. She nudged Kathy with her elbow as she stood up.

"It was nice to meet you, sergeant. Thank you for telling us what happened.'' She started to move away, beckoning Kathy to follow with a jerk of her head. "We're going to play some tennis to work up an appetite before lunch. Right, Kathy?''

"Er, quite right.'' A somewhat bewildered Kathy followed her out of the lobby.

"Now, what was that all about?'' The sergeant looked at Uncle Jim with a puzzled look. "Why did they suddenly leave like that?''

"I've no idea.'' Uncle Jim was just as mystified.

"Slow down,'' Kathy puffed as she chased after Susan, who was climbing the stairs two and three at a time. "What's eating you, anyway?''

"Didn't you see him?'' She didn't break step as she

swung into their corridor, and continued along to their room.

"See whom?" Kathy flopped on her bed, panting to catch her breath.

"See that sergeant winking at his corporal, then at your Uncle Jim, when he thought that I wasn't looking?" She marched over to the window and looked out across the blue of the lake to the mountains rising up from the water some five miles away. She turned round, resting her elbows on the window ledge. "He didn't take us seriously for one minute!"

"I didn't see him winking. I thought he was being very kind and patient. After all, to him we are no different from millions of other schoolgirls."

"Well I *saw* him, and I'm going to *show* him. We're going to solve this case before he has time to sneeze. Then, let him wink as much as he likes!" Snorting, she left the window, and going to the bedside table took out some sheets of writing paper and a pencil. Sitting down on her bed, she started to draw up a list of questions.

"What about our game of tennis?" Kathy sat up, peering to see what Susan was doing.

"What about it?"

"I thought you said we were going to have a game before lunch." She moved to sit beside her cousin.

"Are you crazy?" Susan stopped writing for a moment as she looked at her. "We've no time for playing games; we've got a case to solve. So just help me answer these questions."

Kathy shook her head in resignation. Here we go again, she thought. Once Sue's got the sleuthing bug, forget everything else.

"Question one. On what dates have these thefts taken place?"

"Just a moment; I'll get my notes." Kathy went to her bedside table drawer and pulled out her notebook once more. "I don't keep a diary, but since you weren't here I made a note each day of what I did, to remind me when I tell you about my extra weeks of holiday." Normally this mild goading would have set Susan off on an amusing tirade, which Kathy would have enjoyed immensely, but now she was much too intent on the case to notice. "Here we are. The first theft took place before I arrived, as I explained to you yesterday. Since I arrived, however, thefts were reported on August first, August eighth, ah . . ." She flipped back through the pages. "Oh yes, July twenty-fifth, and July eighteenth."

"Uh-huh, and yesterday was August twenty-second." Susan jotted down the dates in chronological sequence. She studied them for a few seconds, then suddenly shot a question at Kathy.

"And what about the fifteenth?"

Kathy searched her notes again. "No, there's no record of theft that day."

"Fine, we have clue number one. Look —" Susan turned her paper so that the list of dates was clearly visible "— yesterday was Tuesday, right?" Kathy nodded her agreement. "And for at least four of the five preceding Tuesdays there was a theft. But on Tuesday, August fifteenth, there was none."

"At least, there wasn't one reported," Kathy interjected.

"Good point," Susan admitted. "Whatever the case, there is a clear pattern. All reported thefts took place on a Tuesday. Did your uncle tell you the date of the first one, the one that took place prior to your arrival?"

"No, but let me think for a minute. I came here on a Friday, and for some reason I think it happened two or three days before that." She frowned in concentration, trying to stir her memory. "Oh yes, I remember. Uncle said he couldn't put us in the room he had planned for us, because it was still being investigated. That's right; not being paying guests, we normally would have had one of the rooms facing the hills behind, rather than this one which overlooks the lake. I remember asking how long it had been sealed up, and he said either for two days, or since Tuesday. Frankly I was too busy looking out the window at the marvellous view, thinking how lucky we were to have this room. I just didn't pay attention; I'm sorry."

"Never mind, that's close enough. So now we want to know, why only on Tuesdays?" She lapsed into silence as she worried at the question. Many possibilities flitted through her mind, but she knew too little to accept any one at this time. "Let's press on and answer a few more questions. Perhaps the answers will throw some light on the Tuesday timing." She gnawed at the end of her pencil while she marshalled her thoughts. Then, in a sudden burst of activity, she jotted down a number of questions, reading them out as she did so. "What rooms were robbed? What items were taken? Exactly when were the thefts discovered? Who has access to keys that would open the doors? Were there any changes in the staff?" She thought for a while, but nothing else came to mind.

"Would it help if we knew how long the guests had stayed before the thefts took place?" Kathy offered.

"It might prove useful information." She scribbled a note. "Can you think of any other questions that could throw some light on the crimes? Questions which might prompt some indication of *who* and *how?*"

"Well, it might help if we knew whether the guests had stayed here before, or whether they came from the same city or part of the country."

"Good. We'll check those points as well." Susan jotted down the questions. "The majority of these questions can be answered from the hotel register. Do you think that your Uncle Jim would let us borrow it for an hour or so?"

"Let's go and ask him." Kathy stood up, but when she glanced at her watch she hesitated. "It's nearly lunch time, and he'll be busy watching over the dining room. Let's wait until later when we can catch him on his own."

"Fair enough, we'll do that. But talking of lunch, I'm pretty hungry myself. Let's go and eat."

Kathy just beat her to the door, laughing as she led the way down the corridor. This time she insisted on waiting for the elevator, much to Susan's disgust.

After lunch, when most of the adult guests had made their way to their rooms, or had gone off for afternoon activities, the girls managed to corner Uncle Jim alone in his office. He was very patient answering their many questions, and agreed to allow them to take the register to their room on the clear understanding that it was to be returned to the desk before breakfast the next morning. He also let them take the key to the room that had been robbed the previous day. The guest had moved to another room, and the police had examined it, but only briefly, because it was identical to the other rooms in the hotel. Having left the register in their room, and locked the door, the girls made their way to the fourth floor. It was hardly worth waiting for the elevator. They moved along the corridor, checking the numbers on the doors.

"The rooms are numbered in the same sequence as those on our floor," Kathy remarked. "Even numbers face the rear, and odd numbers look out over the lake."

"Yes, and here's room four one two." Susan fitted the key in the lock and pushed the door wide open, holding out her arm to bar Kathy's way into the room. Then, without further ado, she flopped down on her stomach, feet stretched out into the corridor. "What on earth are you doing now?" Kathy looked down at her.

"The room was probably well worked over by the police, and no doubt cleaned by the staff, but you never know — there may be something they missed." She wriggled until her nose was pressed against the carpet, eyes as close to the floor as she could get them. Then, squinting, she peered along the carpeted floor. Slowly she inched forward into the room until she could see under the bed and other furniture. At last, satisfied, she rose to her feet. "No luck. Only a hair clip, but it was worth the effort." She brushed her clothes.

"Maybe I can come in now?" Kathy didn't wait for an invitation, but stepped over the threshold, closing the door as she did so. "Now let me into your secret. What did you hope to accomplish crawling about on the floor like a baby?"

"Haven't you noticed," Susan asked, "how much easier it is to spot a small object on the floor by getting down to the same level?" She dug in her pocket and, taking out a dime, tossed it on the floor under the table next to the bed. "There, you can see that quite plainly because you know where it is, but turn your back for a moment." Kathy did as she was told. Susan picked up the coin, moved further into the room, and placed it on the floor just below the window. Then, standing so that her shadow fell over the coin, thus stopping it from glinting, she said, "Now tell me where the dime is."

Kathy peered around the room, under the bed, under

the table, under the chair. "I can't see it. Where did you put it?"

"Go back toward the door, and lie on your stomach as I did. Then peer along the carpet with your eye as close to the floor as possible. You'll notice that every little hump and bump will show up very clearly, even something as thin as a dime. You'll have to move forward slowly so that you can see over the bumps."

Kathy lay down, wrinkling her nose at the dusty closeness of the carpet. Then, turning her face to one side, she brought her right eye down to carpet level. Squinting, she swept her eye across the surface. Immediately she spotted the hair clip missed by the cleaner, a match head, and then, as she inched forward, the edge of the dime.

"Ha! There it is." Climbing to her feet she moved forward to pick it up.

"Oh no, you don't! That's mine!" Chuckling, Susan swooped down and retrieved her coin.

"I see what you mean." Kathy pulled a tissue from her pocket and scrubbed her nose to remove the pieces of carpet fluff that threatened to make her sneeze. "I could clearly see a hair clip and a match head, as well as the dime."

"Where? What match? I didn't see that," Susan admitted. She scrutinized the floor, forgetting her own advice, and not lying down.

"There, under the drawers," Kathy indicated.

"Now, that's interesting." Susan took an envelope from her pocket and flipped the match head into it. "See, it hasn't been burned." She tilted the open envelope, moved to the table next to the bed, and looked in the ashtray. "Do you see? The hotel matches are the book type —" she picked up a slim package, holding it so

Kathy could clearly see the hotel crest embossed on the front — "while this unburned match head came from a wooden match. Therefore it came from a match brought into the room from outside."

"Perhaps it belonged to the cleaner, or the guest that was resident in this room," Kathy observed.

"I doubt very much if it belonged to the cleaner." She shook her head. "I'm not saying that a cleaner wouldn't smoke, but if he or she did, I'm quite sure that anything dropped would be picked up. It would be an automatic action. If it was the last guest, we should be able to confirm it later." She sealed the envelope, and slipped it into the back pocket of her jeans. She then started to search the room thoroughly. She opened closets, peered into drawers, and scoured the bathroom that led off the bedroom. The place was bare of any further unusual items. She retrieved the hair clip, placing it in yet another envelope, and then examined the door. She peered closely at the surface around the keyhole, searching for signs of lock picking, but no scratches were visible. Next she looked in the hole that received the door latch to see if it had been blocked by a piece of paper or wood, a well known trick used by thieves who wished to prevent a door from locking when closed, but it was quite clear.

Meanwhile, Kathy moved across to the window. She had watched Susan in action before, and knew that she would next examine the window frame for signs of forced entry.

"See anything?" Susan joined her at the window.

"No, there are no fresh scratches or marks to suggest that the window was opened from the outside." Kathy moved back so that Susan could look closely. "I'm really glad that our room is at the front of the hotel, aren't

you? We have a much nicer view."

Susan looked out of the window at the steep wooded slope rising behind the hotel. It certainly wasn't a view to compare with their own. There was no shining blue of the lake; no cool reflection of distant, snow capped mountains; no slash of yellow beach with colourful umbrellas dotted about. Instead, a drab hillside covered with straggling brush and small trees, climbing to the colder, northern skies. She peered downwards but her view was blocked by the broad window ledge. She unlatched the window and swivelled it open. It was of the design that pivots about a central, horizontal hinge, so that both sides might be easily cleaned from inside the room. Leaning out, she looked downwards to see a row of cars parked on a large paved area; obviously, the guests' parking lot. Twisting her neck to look upwards, she could just see the window ledges of the fifth floor rooms, used for storage, where they projected from the sloping roof. She carefully eased herself back into the room, stretching to relieve the soreness brought about by straining her back against the window frame.

"Fine, I don't think that there's anything more for us to see in here for the present. Let's go back to our room and start work." She latched the window and, with Kathy leading the way, they returned to their own quarters on the third floor.

After a successful foraging trip to the reception desk to obtain some blank sheets of paper and felt pens, and a side excursion to the kitchen to pick up "sustaining refreshment", as Susan described it, they were ready to commence.

Susan taped a large sheet of white paper to the mirror of the dressing table. With a felt tipped pen she drew a number of vertical lines, and, with the help of Kathy, constructed a historical record of the thefts, and the arrivals and departures of the guests. After an hour of hard work it was finished, and the girls sprawled on their beds to survey their handiwork.

"Okay, let's recap what has happened." Susan ticked off the points on her fingers as she enumerated them. "Firstly, we know that all of the thefts took place on a Tuesday."

"Correction," Kathy interjected. "Were *reported* on a Tuesday."

"That's right. We'll have to find out if the guests reported the thefts immediately." She shook her head. "No, that's not what I mean. We need to know if it was possible for any length of time to elapse between the theft taking place and the guest discovering it."

Kathy looked puzzled for a moment, but then her brow cleared. "Oh! You mean, for instance, were all of the guests immediately aware of their losses on returning to their rooms, because they had last seen the stolen articles just before they left their rooms earlier?" She looked puzzled, bewildered by her own words.

Susan chuckled, "You seem to have as much trouble as I did explaining yourself, but I think that we both know what the other is thinking. Let's press on." She bounced from the bed and made a note on the sheet of paper. "Secondly, all of the rooms were on the north side of the building, the side facing the hills, rooms 308, 412, 314, 326, 420, and 412. Thirdly, we know that on all occasions only money was taken, although in several cases valuable jewellery was also in the room at the same time as the money. Fourthly, there appears to be no connection between the guests who were robbed. Their home towns are as far apart as Montreal and Winnipeg. Fifthly, in addition to the room key that each guest has, there are two master keys."

"Right, one of which is on Uncle Jim's key ring, and the other held by the head porter." Kathy thought it about time to add her contribution to the proceedings. "We also know that in every case the guest had booked in the preceding Saturday or Sunday."

"That's correct," Susan nodded, "and — I think this must be important in some way — all of the guests stayed here last summer, three of them for at least the last three years."

"We certainly seem to have a lot of facts, but will they be of any use to us?"

"You mustn't ignore anything in an investigation," Susan reminded her. "Now, what else do we know?" They were both busy with their own thoughts for several seconds, wracking their brains. "Oh yes, according to your uncle, there have been no changes in staff during the last year, except for the addition of temporary summer help, mainly students. There are three of them, and none of them worked here before this summer. One works as a porter, carrying the bags in for the guests — and out again, of course. Another works in the kitchen as general help, and the third is a room maid."

"They must be our prime suspects, I guess?" Kathy posed the question.

"They may be suspects, but I don't think that we can say they are the prime suspects at this time." Susan rolled over onto her front. "You have to be very careful at the start of an investigation not to pin labels on people, or to become fixed on a particular clue. Otherwise you'll find that you tend to twist the facts to suit a theory, with the danger of missing other points which could lead you to the true culprit."

"In other words, we must keep open minds until we

know as much as we can possibly learn?'' Kathy nodded her understanding, her words being more of a statement than a question. "Then, what about the rest of the staff?''

"It could well be one of the regular staff, but as they are all local residents, and have worked here for years, I think the likelihood of it being one of them is pretty remote. But, as I said, we mustn't jump to any conclusions, and they must remain as suspect as anybody else.''

"Perhaps the thief is another guest!'' Kathy burst out as the thought flashed across her mind.

"Now, that's a good point; a very good point. If it were another guest, it would have to be one who has lived at the hotel since before the date of the first robbery. Let's look in the register.''

The girls worked through the names of the occupants of each of the hotel's ninety-eight rooms, listing those who had stayed at the hotel for more than five weeks.

"That's a relief.'' Kathy sat back with a sigh of satisfaction. "Only four who have resided in the hotel for the whole period.''

"Yes, and none that were here earlier, and have since returned. I guess it would be just too much of a coincidence if we had found somebody who had been here right through the time span except for the week when there was no theft.''

"Well,'' Kathy stretched, yawning as she did so, "I don't know about you, but I'm tired and ready for my bed. All this brain work makes me very sleepy.''

"Mm, it's probably a good time to stop.'' Susan placed her notes on the bedside table. "Tomorrow we'll set about answering some of our questions. At least we now know that all of the thefts took place from rooms in the rear of the building, only money was taken, even though other valuables were left lying about and, from what Uncle Jim said this afternoon, it seems that the guests always found the rooms just as they were left, with the door locked. Let's go to bed."

Thursday, at Kathy's insistence, the girls spent their time on the lake in a small sail boat owned by Uncle Jim. One of the students who worked at the hotel helped them rig and launch it.

"Thank you . . ." and Kathy paused to learn the student's name.

"Gerry. Gerry Braun," the student said.

"Thank you then, Gerry," Susan smiled as the boat caught the breeze and drew away from the shore.

Not particularly interested in athletic pastimes, Susan was a novice, and it was Kathy's turn to be the teacher. Fortunately both girls were strong swimmers, and they were in no danger despite the numerous times they found themselves in the water when Susan took the tiller. They took a packed lunch with them, luckily carried in a watertight, buoyant picnic cooler. It was quite late in the evening when they at last tied up at the dock just across the road from the hotel. After dinner an interesting television programme took their attention, and it was two very tired young ladies who dragged themselves up to bed at the ridiculously early hour of ten o'clock. Just before turning out the light Susan picked up her notes, but she was just too fatigued to concentrate, resolving to make an early start on the case the following morning.

"Galloping goldfish! Look at the time!" Susan scrambled out of bed.

"Eh? Whasamatta?" Kathy roused herself, dragging one eye open against the bright light as Susan opened the drapes.

"It's nearly nine, you lazy layabout," Susan exclaimed. "Come on! Shake a leg, or we'll be too late for breakfast." It took a little persuasion, including a very wet towel in the face, but eventually Susan had her cousin marching down to the dining room. Gradually the sky darkened, and it was apparent that it would be a rainy day. They had just finished breakfast when the skies opened, the rain falling in solid sheets. Uncle Jim was most apologetic, almost as if he were responsible for the unseasonable weather.

"I'm sorry that it is turning out to be such a miserable day. It's very rare for us to have weather like this during the summer."

"We'll find plenty to do. Don't worry about it, Uncle," Kathy rushed to reassure him.

"Yes, we'll get back to our investigation," Susan told him. "Besides, I need at least a day to recover from all that hard work of yesterday." She moved her shoulders with a grimace. "I didn't think that messing about in a boat would result in so many sore muscles." Her words and facial contortions brought smiles to their faces.

In answer to his question, the girls told Uncle Jim of their progress in their investigations, gaining much useful information in return. They left him and returned to their room, well supplied with soft drinks, chocolate bars, potato chips and other goodies.

Comfortably settled, with the timetable once more taped to the mirror and with notes in hand, Susan went over their progress to date.

"Only on Tuesdays; in rooms facing the back; only money taken, and only stolen from guests who had checked in on the Sunday immediately preceding the theft." She raised her eyebrows at Kathy as if asking for her confirmation.

"But remember, one Tuesday was missed," Kathy reminded Susan. "Also, the rooms were all on the third and fourth floors, and the doors were always found locked."

"Not only that, but from what Uncle Jim told us this morning, the windows were also closed and latched, as you would expect with air-conditioning in the rooms."

"I think that we can eliminate the four long term guests as possible suspects. They're all on the first or second floor," Kathy observed. Then she chuckled. "From what Uncle Jim told us, they're all about eighty, and I can't see any of them speeding around corridors, nipping in and out of other guests' rooms, and racing up and down stairs."

"The only clues that we have are one hair clip, and one unburned wooden match head," said Susan. "I can see why the police have made so little progress." She sat in thought for two or three minutes, absent-mindedly nibbling a potato chip. "We have to develop a theory that fits the facts. How would you go about robbing five locked rooms, so that the doors and windows were found to be in the same locked condition afterwards?"

"How would you know which rooms to rob?" Kathy countered the question with one of her own.

"Fine, let's start there. If you remember, all of the guests who were robbed had also stayed here last summer. That may be just a coincidence but, on the other hand, it may not. Perhaps somebody knows, or has some way of finding out, that these particular people always carry cash instead of travellers' cheques." Susan pursed her lips as she thought. "But how could the thief find that information? We know that the guests come from different parts of the country, so that rules out knowledge in advance."

"Could it be that when they pay their bill, they pay in cash, and that's the tip-off?" Kathy offered a possible explanation.

"That's something we can ask Uncle Jim, but I would think that most people pay in advance, by cheque. After all, this is a resort hotel, and people have to book ahead of time to make sure of their rooms. Again, I think that guests pay in advance in cash only if they are passing through, and staying for just one night. Otherwise it would be more likely they would pay their bill when it was time to leave."

"That's true. So how else could somebody know that these guests carried large sums of cash, rather than using credit cards, for instance?" Kathy sighed as she shrugged her shoulders. This really was turning out to be a complicated puzzle.

"How about this?" Susan's eyes gleamed. "All of the rooms face the rear, right?" Kathy nodded. "And all of the rooms are overlooked by the hills. I'll bet that with a good pair of binoculars you could see into every room on that side from up in the trees."

"Then you could see what people were unpacking, and what they put in the closets and drawers." Kathy sprang up and looked out of the window. "Darn this rain! We'll get soaked to the skin if we go climbing up that hill now."

"That's all right; we'll go when it stops. We still have a number of questions to answer. Let's assume, for the moment, that the thief spies on the guests to locate the most promising rooms to rob. The next question is, how does he get into the rooms and out again without being discovered?"

"We can take it that as a result of the precautions taken after the first robbery, he doesn't use one of the pass keys." Kathy had in mind the long discussion they had had with her uncle on this very point. The pass keys were never out of the possession of Uncle Jim and the head porter. Suddenly her face dropped in consternation.

"You don't suppose for a moment that it could be either Uncle Jim or the porter, do you?" It was unthinkable.

"No, no." Susan shook her head firmly. "It just wouldn't make any sense. Both of them have lived here for years, and it just isn't reasonable to consider that they would risk their jobs and future pensions for the few hundred dollars involved."

"Whew! That's a relief. For one ghastly second . . ." She shook her head in disbelief, her brain grappling for some other possibility. "Could the thief have taken an impression of one of the keys some time ago, and then later had another one made?"

"It's a possibility," Susan admitted, "although making a key from a wax impression is not as easy as fiction would have you believe. Still, let's assume that he did. That means that it would have to be a member of the staff, and one who would not raise suspicion if seen in the corridors."

"That narrows the choice of suspects to the room maids."

"And the porters."

"And the restaurant staff, because they often deliver meals to the guests' rooms," Kathy pointed out.

"And the maintenance staff. I think there are so many possibilities that the only way to catch this thief is to nab him on the job." Susan threw down her pencil in frustration. She picked up a coke, and after a long drink walked across to the window. "Good! The rain isn't as heavy now." Stooping, she peered up at the clouds. "I

do believe that the clouds are breaking up. Perhaps we'll be able to go out this afternoon. If nothing else, a good walk will help clear our brains, and give us some new ideas."

"Let's go down to lunch. It's nearly noon." Kathy was getting a little bored. "We can have a game of table tennis if we're too early. Come on." She started for the door.

"Just a moment." Susan was closely examining the window frame. Two or three times she swung the window open and closed. One eyebrow climbed as a satisfied gleam came to her eye. She nodded to herself in answer to an unspoken question.

"What are you doing now?" Kathy was impatient to go.

"Oh, er . . . nothing." Susan straightened up and followed her cousin to the door, picking up her wallet from the table as she did so. "You can't be too careful, you know!"

After lunch the rain clouds moved away and weak sunlight streamed down upon the lake, turning it from a sullen gray to a pale blue. Susan and Kathy borrowed a pair of binoculars from Uncle Jim and, dressed in their oldest clothes, set off scrambling up the wooded slopes behind the hotel. Ten minutes of hard climbing later they found themselves level with the hotel roof. They had some difficulty in finding a spot where the trees and tall bushes did not obstruct their view, but eventually they settled in a small clearing from which the whole of the rear of the hotel was clearly visible. Putting the binoculars to her eyes, Susan twisted the focusing wheel. Suddenly she found herself looking with surprising clarity directly into one of the rooms on the fourth floor. It was almost as if she were standing on a ladder propped against the window ledge. Quite clearly she could see every detail inside the room. She swept the glasses down to the next floor, quickly moving them again as she spotted a man changing his suit.

"If we have to move into one of the rooms on this side, just make sure I close the drapes before undressing, will you?" She passed the glasses to Kathy. "See how clearly you can see into those rooms?"

Kathy took the glasses from her and put them to her eyes. After an initial problem with the focus she agreed, "You really can see everything in the rooms, can't you?" She moved to look into another room. "Look, there's a lady reading in that room. I can almost make out the title of the book." She took the glasses down from her face. "Sort of a funny feeling, spying on people when they don't know you are watching them, isn't it?"

"Hey! Look what I've found." Susan stooped, pointing. There, half hidden by fallen leaves, were three burnt matches.

"That proves your theory then, doesn't it?" Kathy glowed with excitement.

"No, it doesn't prove that a watcher comes up here to spy on the guests, or that he is our thief. It might just be that a guest or staff member came up here for a walk, having absolutely nothing to do with the robberies."

"A walk!" Kathy snorted. "More likely to be mountain climbing."

Susan grinned as she agreed. "Even so, we mustn't jump to conclusions." She picked up the small pieces of charred wood and wrapped them in a tissue before buttoning them in her shirt pocket. Taking the binoculars from Kathy, she spent several minutes closely examining the building, paying particular attention to the roof and upper windows. Then, as the sky darkened, and two or three large drops of rain splashed onto the leaves above them, they hurriedly descended to the hotel.

"Uncle Jim, at what times do most guests arrive?" The girls had just finished their dinner, but before returning to their room Susan had several questions to ask.

"What exactly do you mean?" He cocked his head in question.

"Sorry," she chuckled. "I guess I didn't phrase that very well. What I mean is, what day of the week do most people arrive? Is it Friday evening, Saturday or Sunday, for example?"

"Oh, now I understand. Well, during the vacation season most of our guests stay for one, two or three weeks. The week usually starts at noon on Sunday, through to ten o'clock the following Sunday morning. This leaves us a couple of hours to prepare the rooms for the next guests. Actually, very few vacationers arrive before lunch on Sunday, many coming by a train which arrives at two o'clock. We send the hotel bus for them, and it's usually about three before they check in."

"Thanks. Have the police placed the hotel under surveillance on a Tuesday to see if they could spot the thief at work?" Susan voiced the question she had forgotten to ask the previous day.

"Yes, after the second or third robbery — I've forgotten which — they set two policemen to watch, but nothing came of it. In fact, that was one day there was no theft, so perhaps they scared off the burglar."

"That must have been —" Susan consulted her notes "— August the fifteenth."

"Yes, sometime around there."

"One more question, Uncle Jim. Who cleans the windows?"

"Why, er, the porter, usually."

"Is that the head porter, or one of his assistants?"

"It varies, depending on how busy we are, but usually the assistant porters do things like that."

"Um. Well, I think that's all I have for now. Thank you for being so patient, Uncle Jim." Susan nudged Kathy, and they left the office.

"What do you plan to do now?" Kathy asked as she pulled the door closed behind them.

"I want to take another look at the room that was last robbed, and then I'm going to put my theory together."

"Do you know how the thief does it?" Kathy was somewhat confused. They hadn't learned very much of importance, yet the gleam in Susan's eye was a pretty sure indication that she was hot on the scent.

"I'd rather not say just yet but let's admit I am getting a little warmer." Despite Kathy's pleadings, she would say no more.

During the next two days Susan's manner completely mystified Kathy. Early on Sunday morning she had cornered Uncle Jim and quizzed him about the guests expected that day. Did he know any of them from previous visits? Were there any that he could really trust? Would he call any of them good friends? Upon learning that one of them was an old wartime companion, she asked if he would arrange for his friend to be placed in one of the back rooms on the third or fourth floor. Somewhat puzzled, Uncle Jim agreed. Then Susan asked if she could talk to the friend before his luggage was taken up to his room. After the guests had arrived and had lunch, Susan had her conversation, but refused to tell Kathy anything about it. On Monday, with the guest's permission, she visited the room which he now occupied. That evening she asked Uncle Jim if he would arrange for the police corporal or sergeant to come to the hotel but in plain clothes.

This time, at Susan's request, into the small manager's office crowded Uncle Jim, Kathy, Susan, two policemen, and the guest, Mr. Brenner.

"Carry on then, Susan; it's your show." Uncle Jim indicated that she should start her explanation.

"Well, gentlemen . . ." She giggled slightly; being the centre of attention was a bit nerve-wracking, especially when two of the people were policemen. "I think I know how the robberies were committed, but I don't yet know who the thief is. I have one strong suspect, and two minor possibilities. Only by catching the thief in the act can I be absolutely sure who it is."

"Who is your prime suspect?" Uncle Jim asked.

"I'd rather not say at this time. Much better if we catch him in the act. I am quite certain that once again, tomorrow evening, during the dinner hour, one of your guests will report that he has been robbed. In fact, I'm sure that Mr. Brenner will be that guest." She nodded in the direction of Uncle Jim's friend who stood crammed between the filing cabinet and the window. "The reason I asked you all to be here is because I want to set a watch to catch the thief in action."

"We've tried keeping watch before, but nothing happened," Corporal Davis interjected.

"I know, but this time I can tell you exactly which room to watch. You won't be in the same position of trying to cover the whole of the hotel at once."

"If you know that a crime is about to take place," Sergeant Fenton frowned at her, "then it is your duty to advise us right away." He looked at his corporal and winked.

"I intend to tell you!" Susan pursed her lips, angered

again by the sergeant's obvious amusement. "Mr. Brenner's room will be burgled some time between six and eight on Tuesday evening. If you will position a man in the bathroom attached to that room before four o'clock, I am sure that he will surprise the thief as I claim."

"Why in the bathroom? Why not in a room across the corridor?"

"Because the thief will enter the room through the window, and if you are outside the room you will not catch him." Susan said the last five words with some pleasure. She dearly wanted to show this sergeant a thing or two about detection.

"Very well, young lady, I'll hide in the bathroom myself. If we catch the thief as you claim we will, I'll certainly expect to receive a full explanation of how you obtained this advance knowledge."

Without more ado the meeting broke up. Despite Kathy's pleadings, Susan would say no more, except to offer one clue.

"Take a close look at our window."

On Tuesday evening, Susan, Kathy, and Uncle Jim went to dinner early. By seven-fifteen they were settled in his office, waiting. Susan sat back, outwardly quite serene, but inwardly her stomach was churning with anxiety. She had wracked her brains for possible ways in which the thefts could be accomplished, and all the facts available pointed to only one possible method. She was sure that it was an "inside job", that a member of the staff was guilty, and she was ninety-nine per cent certain that she knew the identity of the culprit. She looked at her watch; nearly seven-thirty. Any minute now, unless she had made a complete mess of it! She sent up a little prayer. Just at that moment there was a tap on the door.

"Come in." Uncle Jim half rose in his chair as the door opened, but he sank back again when he saw that it was his old friend, Mr. Brenner. "Oh! It's only you, Peter; I thought it might be Sergeant Fenton."

"Well, young lady —" Mr. Brenner looked at Susan, a slight smile playing round his lips — "I guess you're pretty nervous by now, eh?" Then, at Susan's nod, he continued. "Waiting's over!" With a flourish he threw wide the door and there, standing on the threshold, was a triumphant Sergeant Fenton, and a woebegone looking youth.

"Why, Gerry! You?" Uncle Jim shook his head in disbelief.

"That's right; Gerry Braun. I caught him right in the act, just as he ciimbed in through the window."

Susan let out a pent-up sigh of relief; she was very happy, but, at the same time, quite sad. While it was always pleasurable to crack a case, it was also depressing to realize that some people preferred to live outside the law. This boy had no reason to steal. He was only part-time help for the season, but he would have earned more than enough money for his needs as a student.

"You were right, Susan." For the first time the sergeant addressed her by name. "I shall be back in an hour, and then perhaps you'll let me in on your little secrets?" His glance travelled over the other people in the office, and with a wink in Kathy's direction, he backed out, taking his prisoner with him.

Much later that evening, after the sergeant had returned, they settled themselves comfortably in the lounge. One last look at her notes, and Susan was ready to explain her theories which had led to the successful conclusion of the case.

"Because all of the thefts were on the third and fourth floors, I figured that the thief probably entered the rooms from the outside, possibly by sliding down a rope from the roof, or a higher window. I became even more convinced of this when I saw that the ground to the rear of the hotel was taken up by the guests' parking area. Although it would take a lot of nerve to slide down a rope in broad daylight, the danger of being seen was not nearly as great as it would be if the thief were to prop a ladder against the wall and climb up. Most of us could hardly miss seeing a ladder propped against the wall, but few people look up sufficiently to notice a rope hanging from a window or a roof." The sergeant nodded his agreement. "I eliminated the possibility of the robberies being committed by the thief's entering through the door because it was just too obvious. After all, with three or four floors above the ground, and only one door to the room, there would be absolutely no escape route should the guest return to his or her room unexpectedly. If the burglaries had taken place on the ground floor, or even the second, entry through the door could not be discounted, because the thief could always jump through the window to escape. Having established that point in my mind, I next concentrated on possible methods that the thief might have used to gain access to the rooms, even though the windows were reportedly locked. Fortunately, the thief left me a good clue when he robbed room four hundred and twelve last Tuesday."

"What clue? I didn't see one!" Kathy broke in.

"Ah! But you did." Susan turned to her. "If you remember, I gave you a hint; I said to take a look at our window. The screws holding the latch were covered with paint, as one would expect in a hotel that had been decorated a number of times during its life; however, the screws in room four-twelve have paint removed from the screwdriver slots and now so do those in the room occupied by Mr. Brenner.''

"So that's why you wanted to look in his room yesterday!" Kathy was still puzzled. "But supposing the screws had been removed and replaced. How could the thief do this from the outside?"

"He didn't, of course." Susan continued with her explanation. "The windows are cleaned by the porters. You remember I asked Uncle Jim about that?" Kathy nodded. "Well, what happened was that when Gerry Braun cleaned the windows on Monday he removed the screws, replacing them with others that were cut short so that only one or two threads remained. A good strong push on the window would be sufficient to pop out the screws, and the window would swing open. After he had taken the money he replaced the fake screws with those which he had removed earlier.

"How did he lock the window from the outside?" the corporal asked with a quick glance at his sergeant.

"If the latch is balanced so that it is almost closed on windows like these, which open by swinging on a horizontal pivot and have a simple bar type catch, then slamming the window causes the catch to drop into place."

"I see. Very clever!" The corporal nodded his admiration.

"Well, that's about all there is to tell. Sunday afternoons the thief — Sorry, Gerry — climbed up into the trees behind the hotel. There, equipped with a pair of binoculars, he watched newly arrived guests unpacking. It was easy for him to spot those who placed a large sum of money in the drawer or under the bed. Then, on Monday, as he went round cleaning windows, he

changed the screws as I described. The next day — Tuesday — when most of the guests were at dinner, he would slip down a rope from the storage rooms on the fifth floor, push open the window, and take the money.''

"Why didn't he take the money on Mondays?" Mr. Brenner asked.

"I'm sure that on Tuesday most of the porters were off." She looked at Uncle Jim for confirmation, and at his nod she continued. "On Monday nights he went up to the storage rooms and hid, remaining there all day Tuesday. This way he always had a good alibi; he could claim that he left the hotel on Monday evening, and as no one saw him, there was no evidence to the contrary. The time that you kept watch —" she looked at Sergeant Fenton — "I suspect that he got advance warning of your intentions, and just didn't bother to stay in the hotel. I'm sure that if you go up to the storage rooms you'll find some evidence of his stay there; probably cigarette butts and matches.''

"But why did you suspect young Gerry in particular?" Uncle Jim voiced the question that was puzzling Kathy, not to mention the others.

"Once I'd come up with my theory I studied the porters. Two of them smoke, but only Gerry seemed to have a preference for wooden matches rather than the hotel book-type. Kathy and I found the end of a broken match in room four-twelve, and we also found burned matches up on the hill. I was sure it had to be Gerry."

"Well done, Susan. I must say that catching the thief has taken a load off my shoulders." Uncle Jim sat back, a contented smile on his lips.

"Why did you get involved in this, Susan?" Mr. Brenner asked.

"She's always been an amateur detective," Kathy

answered.

"No, the reason this time was that Sergeant Fenton didn't take us seriously." She looked at the policeman accusingly.

"I did take you seriously. Honest I did!" Sergeant Fenton said with some indignation. Then he winked.

"See what I mean?" Susan shrieked.

"See what?" The sergeant was completely puzzled.

"You winked again!" she accused.

"Ahem!" Uncle Jim coughed to draw her attention. "I think you should know that Sergeant Fenton was slightly wounded in the last war, and it has left him with a slight twitch, which many people mistake for a wink."

"Oh dear!" Susan blushed furiously. Kathy almost fell from her seat as she rolled around, unable to suppress her mirth. The others, including Sergeant Fenton, also burst out laughing. After a few seconds of complete confusion Susan joined them, almost going into hysterics when the Sergeant gasped, "A nod is as good as a wink, eh?"

Susan Super Sleuth and
The Careless Courier

hanks for the fantastic holiday, Joanna.'' Susan hugged her friend with her forearms, hands full of carry-on luggage. The teenagers beamed at each other as they stood among the swirling crowds of tourists at Amsterdam's International Airport.

"No, it is I who must thank you, Susan.'' The Dutch girl smiled as she went on. "I had some fear that we would not — how do you say it — 'hit it off?' ''

"So did I,'' Susan grinned back. "As pen pals we certainly had a lot in common, but we had no way of knowing whether we would become friends when we met.''

"But we are friends, are we not?''

"You bet! I'm really looking forward to next year when you'll come to visit me.''

Slowly they moved forward with the line of travellers toward the entrance of the departure lounge. All too quickly it was Susan's turn to pass through the barrier. One more quick hug, a moment of sadness; then with wide smiles they parted.

"Hi there. Did you have a good vacation?" The Canadian accent had a warm ring to it. Efficiently the Canadian Pacific attendant flipped through Susan's ticket and passport. "Have a good flight."

Nodding her thanks, Susan passed through the metal detecting equipment and into the departure lounge. One of the last to arrive, she saw that waiting passengers occupied all the seats. Carefully stepping over out-stretched legs, she made her way to the farther end of the room and, placing her bag on the floor, propped herself comfortably against the wall for the short wait before boarding.

Idly her eyes roamed over the waiting passengers. The heavy rucksacks, threadbare jeans and unkempt hair of several other teenagers travelling alone or in pairs were indicative of hard living and showed that they had tramped through Europe. There was a mixed crowd of holiday makers, husbands and wives, some with small children, and here and there new Canadians whose mixed emotions of excitement and regret flitted across their faces as they strained to see relatives, now barely visible, and mouthed their farewells through the glass wall. Two Arabs stood in one corner, flowing white robes throwing their black eyes and beards into sharp prominence as they waited silently, close to the boarding exit. Susan smiled to herself as she noticed an ill-matched couple seated directly in front of her: an older lady, grey hair awry, sat inelegantly, one knee crossed over the other, avidly talking to a small nervous man on her left. They were apparently strangers, yet she rummaged in her large handbag, triumphantly producing two or three photographs which she insisted he examine. The man twisted his head from one side to the other, eyes nervously darting about as if he were seeking a good excuse to leave his seat. On the other side of the lady sat an Indian gentleman, his bright turban providing a splash of warm colour in the waiting room. He held a newspaper high in front of his face, an effective means of discouraging the lady should she attempt to force her attentions upon him.

Susan eased her shoulders against the wall, shuffling her feet slightly as she moved. Inadvertently her foot touched that of a man standing beside her. She looked up and apologized as he grunted and quickly moved his own foot away. She noticed that he wore a priest's collar, and was surprised at the fierce scowl with which he greeted her words. He moved further away and Susan wrinkled her nose at his bad manners.

"There you are, my girl!"

Startled, she turned her head just as a man thumped a flight bag onto the floor, just missing her foot.

"Why, Uncle Ted!" She was completely taken by surprise. "What are you doing here? I didn't know you were coming to Holland."

"I arrived only two days ago for an emergency meeting with my colleagues here. Your mother told me before I left that you should be on this flight. I'm glad I spotted you before boarding."

"Perhaps we can sit together on the plane; it's such a long boring flight next to an uninteresting person. With you here, I'm sure we'll have lots to talk about." Uncle Ted supressed a smile. Knowing Susan as he did, he had no doubt as to who would be doing all the talking. "You'll be able to tell me all about your conference," Susan went on. "What was it about this time? Dope

smuggling? International fraud? Murder?'' Her eyes sparkled as she rattled off the questions.

Uncle Ted was a policeman, and his work fascinated Susan. Her naturally inquisitive mind and logical brain were well attuned to detection. Amused, he rolled his eyes upwards in mock despair at her words.

"Here we go again."

Just then the public address speakers instructed the passengers to board the large orange airplane. Picking up their hand luggage, Susan and Uncle Ted turned in the direction of the door. As they did so Uncle Ted's bag swung out, accidentally hitting the stick held by the grey-haired lady, sending it clattering to the floor. Susan darted forward to pick it up, placing it in the lady's hand as her uncle apologized for his clumsiness. Susan grasped the woman's arm, helping her to her feet; then she and her uncle stood back, allowing the older person to precede them through the door and up the ramp to the aircraft.

Fortunately a stewardess easily arranged for a helpful youth travelling alone to exchange seats with Susan, and within a few minutes she and her uncle were side by side, ready for take off, seat belts already fastened.

"That was very nice, thank you." Susan passed her tray to the stewardess and, folding her small table into the back of the seat in front, sat back and gazed out the window at the sea far below. Quickly tiring of the view, she turned to Uncle Ted.

"Are you going to tell me about your conference, or was it one of those mysterious, hush-hush affairs?" she asked.

"No, not really what you might call top-secret, but still quite confidential." He kept his face perfectly straight as he stole a quick glance at her from the corner of his eye and continued, "I certainly shouldn't discuss it with just anybody who expresses interest, you know."

"What a nerve!" Susan burst out. "I'm not just anybody, I'm . . ." She broke off, snorting, as Uncle Ted lost the fight not to smile, and grinned widely. "Oh, you! You're just pulling my leg," and she smiled back. "Come on, Uncle, tell me all about it. Please?" she wheedled.

"O.K." He waited while the stewardess served him a second cup of coffee, and then said, "During the last year or so the incidence of diamond smuggling has increased alarmingly. The purpose of my visit was to meet with members of the police at Amsterdam, and to set up a schedule of meetings for the future. A kind of familiarization trip, you might say."

"Why is it so difficult to catch the smugglers? Surely you could screen international travellers to see who keeps going back and forth to Amsterdam?" She loosened her seat belt, inching round to face her uncle.

"They're much too clever for that. Many smugglers are ordinary people — say vacationers — who carry diamonds for a fee. You see, many people think there is nothing terribly wrong with smuggling. They look upon it as a game, not realizing that it is a very serious crime which can result in a lengthy jail term."

"Oh! I thought that real diamond smugglers used professional couriers. You know, false bottomed suitcases, hollow heeled shoes; that sort of thing."

"Good heavens, no! That's not to say that items may not be smuggled that way, but the customs officers are up to such tricks; they're far too risky. More likely a young family on holiday or a business man on a sales trip will be approached to carry jewels with them when they return home. You'd be surprised at the hiding places that are used.''

"Give me some 'for instances,' uncle.'' She found the topic fascinating.

"All right. For example, hidden inside a baby's diaper, a doll, a camera, a hollow book, or sewn in the lining of a garment. The possibilities are endless.'' He raised his shoulders expressively.

"Mmm, I see what you mean,'' she said, nodding her understanding. "Certainly it would be impossible to search every piece of luggage, clothing, gift, book, and so on.'' She started to chuckle. "Can you imagine how mothers would react if their babies were 'de-diapered'?''

Her uncle's laugh boomed out over her own chuckle.

"So almost anybody on this plane could be illegally carrying diamonds at this moment?'' Susan said the words quietly as her eyes ranged along the length of the fuselage. Undoing her seat belt she rose and, crouching to avoid bumping her head on the overhead luggage rack, sidled past her uncle and into the aisle. Her imagination was in full flight, and rather than moving to the washrooms in the rear of the aircraft, just three rows back, Susan walked the length of the passenger compartment to the front. Thus, when she returned, she would have the opportunity of examining all the passengers.

As she moved forward along the narrow aisle she was suddenly stopped in her tracks as a man stepped out in front of her. It was the small, nervous looking gentleman whom she had last seen cornered in the departure lounge by the little old lady. He turned his head quickly to look at her before reaching up to the luggage rack to take down a container of duty-free liquor. Without apologizing he hurried toward the forward washrooms. Inadvertently he kicked a foot protruding into the aisle as he passed by, and Susan was close enough to hear the owner snarl as he pulled it in, "Clumsy fool! Why don't you watch where you're going?" The small incident hardly seemed to warrant such an outburst, and Susan was astounded to see it was the priest who had spoken so angrily. As she passed his seat she looked at him closely. His lips were drawn into a thin line, brows creased in an ill-tempered frown as their eyes met momentarily. When she reached the washrooms, Susan found them both occupied, and while waiting she talked briefly with the stewardesses busy in the tiny galley. She stood back as one of them moved past her, a tray with four coffees in her hand, destined for the cockpit. For perhaps thirty seconds Susan had a tantalizing glimpse of the cramped aircrew cabin. Masses of dials, gauges, levers and wheels seemed to occupy every inch of wall and ceiling.

The stewardess backed out with the empty tray and, smiling apologetically at Susan, snapped the door closed behind her. At that moment the sign on the foremost washroom door clicked from "occupied" to "vacant", and the Indian with the bright turban squeezed passed Susan. Accidentally a fold of the turban snagged a protrusion, threatening to pull it from his head. His hands flew up to stop it from being dislodged, but not in time to avoid its being pulled askew. Brusquely, with both hands holding it in place, he pushed back into the washroom. With a small sigh of resignation Susan settled back to wait again, but almost immediately the other washroom was vacated by the small man carrying his duty-free liquor bottle. Without a glance at her he set off for his seat, and she slipped through the narrow door. She wrinkled her nose; the smell of alcohol was almost overpowering. She found the exhaust fan switch and flipped it on to change the air.

Letting herself out of the small compartment Susan found several people lined up patiently waiting. The two Arabs stood talking quietly, their white robes gleaming in the shadows. A group of three students clustered behind them, and Susan could not help overhearing their conversation as she moved past. She slowed as one said, ". . . I hide it in my sock. I know that it's an obvious place to look, but it's still the safest spot."

Susan smiled at her suspicions and moved on when another replied, "I've nothing left to hide. I ran out of money three days ago."

Two stewardesses dispensing refreshments were slowly moving toward the rear of the plane, and blocked the aisle with their trolley. Susan waited, moving patiently along behind them, taking this as a natural opportunity to study the other passengers at her leisure. Many of them, especially the elderly, had settled down to take an after lunch nap. Others were reading books and newspapers; some were doing crossword puzzles; others were gazing out of the windows at the fairyland scene of billowing cloud tops far below. Here and there a parent was engaged in entertaining a child. Susan almost bumped into the stewardesses as they stopped suddenly, when the progress of the trolley was halted by a walking stick protruding into the aisle. Susan smiled, recognizing the little old lady, her grey head bobbing up and down as she talked to — or rather at — her neighbour. She apologetically retrieved the stick, declining the stewardess's offer to place it in the rack above. Susan looked down as she passed by, to see her once again showing her photographs . . .

". . . and there are my daughter's children on the beach near Rotterdam . . ."

Slowly the trolley was moved along to where Uncle

Ted sat, head back, mouth slightly open, eyes closed, comfortably dozing.

"Eh! Wha'sat?" He woke up as she tried to slip past to her window seat without disturbing him.

"Sorry, Uncle Ted. I tried not to wake you."

"That's quite all right. I wasn't sleeping, but just resting my eyes," he protested, stretching and yawning. He glanced at his watch. "Less than three hours from now we should be landing at Toronto." Leaning forward he peered outwards and down. "Yes, you see the cloud sheet ending? We're just coming up to the coast."

Susan followed his gaze; it was possible to discern some five miles below the rugged dividing line between the grey of the sea and the deeper grey-brown of the Labrador coast. She turned her eyes back toward her uncle and spoke in a low voice.

"I've been thinking. Do the crew members pass through customs just like the passengers?"

"Oh, yes. Why do you ask?"

"Just wondering. They travel back and forth all the time, and it seems likely that any who were dishonest would have endless opportunities to smuggle. You know, familiarity might result in their not being scrutinized closely." She thought for a moment, and then continued, "But then, of course, that would be just as obvious to the customs officers."

"That's right, and the airlines are very careful in their employee selection. It's not impossible that they might hire an individual who may later engage in smuggling, but professional pride among aircrew members tends also to be a strong self-policing factor."

Susan nodded her understanding and said, "Changing the subject, do diamond smugglers ever travel in disguise?"

"Occasionally. When a particularly large shipment is made, it may be considered too risky to use an amateur, and an experienced courier might be employed. Then, because we know many of the criminals in the business, one might well pose as somebody else." He looked at her with twinkling eyes. "I suppose you've examined every passenger, eh, Super Sleuth?" Susan blushed slightly. "Did you spot any doubtful characters?"

She returned his smile but then became quite serious. "As a matter of fact I did — several — but I've whittled the number down to one real possibility."

"And who is that?" He raised his eyebrows questioningly.

"I'd rather not say just yet; I want to observe a little longer. If I confirm my suspicions I'll tell you before we reach the customs area."

Uncle Ted did not press her. He had witnessed Susan's detective skills in action several times and was content to wait.

They hurtled westward toward Toronto, the muted roar of the rushing air continuing uninterruptedly. Twice more Susan made her way forward to the washrooms, on one occasion almost falling into the lap of the little grey-haired lady when she stumbled as the aircraft encountered a small air pocket. Gradually the aircraft slowed, slipping downwards toward the haze blanketing the earth below. Peering out through the window, Susan could just make out the needle shape of the C.N. Tower, ten miles to the south. The seat belt and no smoking signs lit up. The plane made two or three small wandering turns as the pilot aligned it with the runway. Almost close enough to touch, a cluster of small buildings suddenly flashed beneath the wings. There was a blur of white concrete, scored with black slashes of rubber, followed by a slight bump, and finally the rumble of the wheels as they rolled down the runway. Momentarily the four jets screamed in reverse thrust, quickly slowing the plane's speed, and then they were turning sedately onto the taxi strip, moving toward the terminal buildings. They stopped, jet engines quietening to a whimper.

Along the length of the compartment passengers rose to their feet, stretching and chattering. Bundles and boxes were retrieved from the overhead racks. Crowding into the aisle, the people began a slow shuffle to the exit. Susan restrained her uncle, holding him back so she could watch one passenger in particular, and they were almost the last to leave. They passed through the exit door, murmuring a word of thanks to the smiling stewardesses, and then travelled along a ramp and down some stairs to the long curving passageway leading to the immigration and customs areas. They took their places with the other passengers, waiting for their luggage to slide down a chute onto a rotating carousel.

"That one there," Susan nudged her uncle, and pointed at one of the passengers. "I think you should arrange for a search."

"Are you quite sure?" he questioned. When she nodded firmly he left her and walked to the nearest customs officer.

Later, Susan and Uncle Ted sat waiting in the chief customs officer's office. The senior official entered and, tossing his cap on the coat rack behind the door, sat down at his desk.

"You were quite right; he soon confessed to being a man when we called a lady officer to conduct a body search. But how did you know?"

"There were a number of clues." Susan stood up and moved about the office as she spoke. "The first thing

that made me suspicious was the way she sat in the lounge at Amsterdam. If you watch older ladies, especially those who need to use a walking stick, they rarely cross their knees. Usually they sit quite primly without crossing their legs at all, or if they do, it is at the ankles. Many older people use a stick because of rheumatic joints, and it would be too painful to lift a knee high enough to cross it over the other. Another indication was her hair. Of course some ladies do have untidy and straggling hair, but even so they usually visit a washroom before landing and brush or comb it into place. This person didn't leave her seat at all throughout the flight. There was also the way in which she — or rather he — held a cigarette. Most ladies, especially older women, hold their cigarettes between the last joints of the third and fourth fingers. He held his cigarette at the bottom of those fingers, curling the fourth finger around the filter.''

"But crossing knees and smoking in a manly way couldn't be enough to make you so certain," the customs officer observed.

"You're quite right," Susan agreed. "It was the photographs that really started me wondering. I know that proud grandparents often show photographs of their grandchildren to other people but this person seemed too insistent, as if playing a role. It was very obvious when he was thrusting them at a man in Amsterdam who couldn't have been less interested. Even the proudest of grandparents would have desisted in the face of such indifference. He did the same thing on the aircraft, but this time I was close enough to see the pictures. He said the photographs were taken in Rotterdam, but at one edge of the background I could see a lattice-like dome shape which is at Ontario Place in Toronto. Obviously he was lying."

"The Cinesphere? The place where they show movies on a huge screen?" Uncle Ted asked.

"Yes, that's it," Susan nodded, and continued. "On another occasion when I went forward, the aircraft lurched and I almost fell on him — sorry, *her* — as she was then! I saved myself by grabbing at the back of the seat in front, but in doing so dropped my comb. Instead of forming a lap with the skirt as a lady would, he caught the comb by snapping his knees together."

"Very observant," Uncle Ted commented, and the customs officer nodded his agreement.

"There was another odd thing when we left the aircraft. When we boarded he carried the walking stick in his left hand. I remember that distinctly because I helped him to his feet." She turned to her uncle. "Do you remember?" He nodded, recalling the scene. "I thought at the time that his arm was unusually firm for an older person. Anyway, as we left the aircraft he used the stick in the other — his right hand. Finally, as we came along that long, curved underground passage, I noticed that on one occasion he made as if to duck under the rail that runs down the middle, but caught himself just in time — obviously not the action one would expect of an old lady." Susan resumed her seat as she ended her explanation and the customs officer slowly nodded his appreciation of her observations. Just then the door opened to admit a junior officer. He shook his head at the senior man.

"Nothing."

"Nothing? No diamonds, no dope, no watches, nothing?"

"Not a thing," the other repeated.

"That's very strange," the senior man mused. "Why

would he bother to travel in disguise like that? Have you determined his true identity?"

"Oh, yes. The Mounties were very helpful there. His name is Charles James White, and he lives in Hamilton, Ontario. They know him very well."

" 'Chalky' White?" Uncle Ted asked.

The other man nodded. "Do you know him?"

"Yes, or rather, I know of him. He's definitely associated with the illicit diamond trade, but we've never managed to catch him with the goods, so to speak."

"Search again," the senior man instructed. "He must be carrying something."

"It must be the walking stick!" Susan burst out.

"The walking stick?" The young man raised his eyebrows.

"Yes, it must be. A walking stick wasn't necessary to the character he was playing, so why carry it?"

"We've already looked at it miss," the junior officer replied.

"Do you think that I might see it?" She looked to the senior officer for permission.

"Of course," he nodded. "Go and get it please, Mike."

While they waited for the young man to return, Susan recounted her other suspicions.

"I suspected the man wearing the priest's collar because he was so rude; not at all what you would expect from a man of the cloth. However the stewardess told me that he had asked for an aspirin on two occasions during the flight to help relieve the pain in his foot. Apparently it is a form of rheumatism which comes on quite suddenly, and he was travelling without medication."

"Certainly a touch of rheumatics is enough to make anybody surly," the officer agreed. "My old grandfather

used to have it from time to time; the pain was excruciating.''

"Then there was the little, nervous man. I was almost convinced that he had partly emptied a bottle of duty-free liquor in the washroom basin, perhaps replacing it with diamonds; the smell was overpowering.''

"Now that would be a great hiding place,'' Uncle Ted broke in. "Duty-free goods such as cigarettes and liquor are rarely examined.''

"Perhaps not,'' Susan replied, "but the stewardess told me that he was a regular passenger — a jockey, I believe — who simply hated flying. Every trip, to calm his nerves, he would visit the washroom several times for a stiff drink.''

"Certainly more expedient and cheaper than repeatedly asking the stewardesses for refreshment, I suppose,'' her uncle observed.

"Then there was the Indian gentleman. I thought perhaps he might have hidden something in his turban, but I had no evidence to support that suspicion. Anyway, by this time I was very suspicious of the little old lady, and decided to concentrate on her.''

"Here we are, sir.'' The young officer returned with the stick, passing it to Susan at his superior's nodded instruction. She examined it carefully, paying particular attention to the handle. It appeared to be a perfectly normal wooden walking stick; a heavily varnished piece of ashwood with a curved handle. She tapped it. It sounded very solid. Holding it up at eye level so that the light from the window reflected along its length, she slowly rotated it. A grunt of satisfaction escaped from Susan's lips.

"Ah, look! See how the light jumps as I turn the stick?'' She held it so that her uncle could see. "I bet that it was split in half along its length, and then glued together again.''

"You suspect that there may be something concealed inside?'' Uncle Ted asked.

"Yes, I do.'' Susan nodded her head emphatically.

"There's one way to find out.'' The senior customs man took the stick from her. "If we're wrong, I'm sure the department funds will extend to buying 'Chalky' a new stick.'' With this he placed one end of the stick on the desk, holding it firmly with his hand. He pushed down on the other end; it bowed under his weight. He pushed harder. Suddenly, with a sharp crack the stick snapped in two and a cascade of gleaming crystals rattled from the severed upper half.

"Holy cow! She was right!'' The young officer gaped in amazement, but Uncle Ted wasn't surprised at all.

Susan Super Sleuth and The Diamond Dilemma

areful, young lady!''

Too late; she staggered as she collided with the man.

"Oops! Sorry, sir." Susan looked up as she apologized; then, as recognition flooded her face, "Oh, it's you, Uncle."

"Good morning, Susan." He steadied her with a large hand.

She glanced behind him at the door from which he had just emerged, noting the name painted on the glass in gilt letters.

"Hodge and Simpson, Wholesale Jewellers." As she read the words aloud an old, familiar gleam lit up her eyes. "Murder, blackmail, embezzlement, or burglary?" she demanded, an impish grin on her lips.

He shook his head, mouth compressed as he fought an answering smile. "I'm not going to tell you. You just run along home like a good little girl, and leave your poor, old, overworked uncle to get on with his work."

"Little girl my foot!" She stamped in pretended anger. Quickly dropping the pose, she thrust her hand under his arm, and snuggling close, peered up at him with widened eyes. "Come on, Uncle Ted. Don't be so mean. You must be on a case, and you know I love a mystery. Let me help you solve it," she wheedled.

"Perhaps it's already solved," he teased.

"I don't think so. You were much too preoccupied to look where you were going when you nearly knocked me over," she answered cheekily, knowing full well that she had caused the collision.

Uncle Ted was a policeman — a detective sergeant in fact — and his work fascinated Susan. She liked nothing better than his discussing cases with her, and on several occasions she had actively helped in their solution. Her involvement remained a closely guarded family secret, for as her uncle often said, "Whoever heard of a police force with a junior teen-age detective?"

"Tell you what! Why don't we go and have a nice milkshake while you tell me all about it?" Susan coaxed him along the sidewalk to a small restaurant in the next building. "You know that discussing a problem often helps to bring it into focus."

"All right, all right," he capitulated with a smile. "I guess you'll give me no peace until I tell you all about it. In you go." He ushered her before him to a corner booth, well isolated from the few other customers.

She waited impatiently as the waitress fussed over them taking their order. About to open her mouth in question, she closed it again as her uncle frowned a warning. The waitress returned with their milk shakes, and two hamburgers added as an afterthought by Uncle Ted; he knew his niece very well. At last she wiped a crumb from her cheek with the back of her hand and drained her glass, pushing it to one side. Leaning across the table with a conspiratorial air, she screwed her features into what she fondly imagined to be a gangster-like scowl, and demanded, "Okay, Uncle Ted. Spill the beans!"

He smiled at her antics. She really looked very funny, but he lifted his briefcase from the floor and placed it on the table between them. He snapped open the lid.

"This is an unusual case . . ." He spoke in a low voice, but immediately broke into a peal of laughter, joined by Susan. "No pun intended, of course." Then he went on. "A quantity of uncut diamonds with a market value of about thirty thousand dollars was taken from a locked safe. There are no signs of forced entry or tampering, and only two people have keys." Susan remained silent, staring at him intently as he explained. "The keys are held by the partners, Mr. Hodge and Mr. Simpson. Both men are adamant in claiming that at no time have the keys left their possession."

"You're suggesting that nobody had the opportunity to take a wax impression and have a duplicate key cut?" It was more of a statement than a question. Her uncle nodded his agreement. She went on. "When was it discovered that the stones were missing?"

"Early this morning; but let me give you all the facts I have collected, in chronological sequence." He opened his notebook and, tearing a blank page from the back, passed it and a pencil to Susan. "Here, you might like to take some notes. Ready?" Susan nodded. "Here we go then. Two days ago, Wednesday, December third, Mr. Hodge returned from California with the diamonds in this box." He took a small cardboard container from his case and offered it to Susan. She quickly drew back her hands. "It's quite all right. The surface is too rough to

show fingerprints," he assured her.

She picked it up, removed the lid and looked inside; it was empty except for a bed of cotton batting. She poked it with her finger, grimacing. "It's damp!" She looked closely at the outside of the box, which was badly stained. "What happened? Did someone try to flush away the evidence?"

"No, no," he answered with a chuckle. "Just before Mr. Hodge put the box away in the safe, he accidentally spilled water over it; his secretary saw it happen. She offered to replace the box, but he was in a hurry to leave for Montreal, and he locked it away in the safe, leaving immediately."

"Where did the water come from? I mean, why was it on the desk in the first place? Did he knock over a vase of flowers?"

"No, it was a glass of water. Apparently the long flight back from California had left him with a headache. He sent his secretary out for some aspirins, and filled the glass with water in anticipation of her coming back with them."

Susan looked at the box once more, a puzzled frown wrinkling her forehead. She turned it over several times before placing it carefully on the table. Cupping her chin in her hands, she prompted, "Continue, Uncle Ted."

"Thursday afternoon, the next day, the other partner, Mr. Simpson, visited the office for an hour or so before leaving for Amsterdam." He paused as Susan raised her eyebrows. Then she shook her head.

"No, it's too obvious; he can't be the thief."

"You're quite right, as usual. Simpson was ill at home on Tuesday and Wednesday with a very bad cold. He left his bed against doctor's orders on Thursday, because he considered the Amsterdam trip very important. As it was, he didn't even reach the airport, collapsing in the taxi on the way. Now he's in the hospital with pneumonia. We traced the taxi driver and determined, without a shadow of doubt, that Simpson had left nothing in the cab. He certainly does not have the diamonds with him in hospital.''

"Who called for the taxi? Do you think there is any possibility of collusion between the taxi driver and Mr. Simpson?''

"No, we are quite sure that there was no prearrangement. The secretary telephoned for the cab. As you know, Thursday is a busy shopping day and taxis are in great demand. She called three companies before she found one willing to dispatch a car for a run to the airport.'' He referred again to his notes. "We investigated the secretary, of course, and I'm convinced that she is not involved. I can't believe that even a topflight actress could fake her emotional condition; she really is quite upset.''

"Did she actually see the gems?''

"She saw them.'' He shook his head slightly. "It's certainly not a case of an insurance claim for nonexistent goods.''

"Did she actually handle them,'' Susan persisted with the line of questioning, "or was she close enough to touch them?''

"Hm.'' Uncle Ted pondered as he tried to recall the interview with the secretary. He flipped through his notes. "Ah, yes! She had just entered the office with the aspirins as Mr. Hodge was about to replace the lid on the box. It was as he was picking up the lid that he accidentally knocked over the glass of water, some of it spilling into the box.'' His eyes twinkled at her as he looked up. "Obviously, you really have poor Mr. Hodge under suspicion.''

"Well, you taught me the first rule of detection," she accused. " 'Assume nothing and question everything.' " She lifted her empty glass, but replaced it with a shake of her head at her uncle's offer of a second milk shake. "When exactly was the theft discovered?"

"This morning, and by both Mr. Hodge and the secretary. But first, let me outline the usual morning routine at Hodge and Simpson's. Each morning the secretary arrives at nine o'clock."

"Excuse me, Uncle. What's her name? The secretary, I mean. It seems rude to keep referring to her as 'the secretary,' as if she were a piece of furniture."

"Miss Smithers; Connie Smithers. Anyway, she arrives at nine. On her way to the office she stops at the post office box and collects the mail. She places it on Mr. Hodge's desk ready for his attention."

"Opened, or unopened?"

"Unopened. Sometimes there may be a registered parcel of low quality stones, and the partners decided long ago that for security purposes one of them should be responsible for opening all mail."

"Because it would be fairer to the secretary." Susan nodded her understanding. This method ensured that no other staff member would be under suspicion should it be found that a letter or package did not contain what it was supposed to.

"Of course," Uncle Ted continued, "more valuable gems are sent by courier. To continue, Mr. Hodge usually arrives before nine-fifteen, closely followed by Mr. Simpson when he is in town. As soon as Mr. Hodge reaches his office, it is his practice to open the mail, while Miss Smithers sits ready to take dictation."

Susan listened intently, occasionally making a note, but relying mainly on her orderly mind, filing information away ready for instant retrieval as needed. She stared unblinkingly as he continued.

"This morning Mr. Hodge found this envelope in the mail." He reached into the case, and passed her an ordinary foolscap envelope. "It held nothing but this photograph." He passed it to her. "There were no fingerprints on it, but there is a crudely printed message on the back."

She examined the envelope closely. The typewriter used to type the address appeared to have no marked irregularities but an expert would no doubt be able to identify the machine should it ever be located. The envelope had been slit open with a letter opener, Susan noticed. Taking a nail file from her pocket, she raised her eyebrows at her uncle for permission; at his nod, she carefully peeled away the severed flap, breathing into the seam to loosen the glue. Borrowing his magnifying glass, she peered at the uncovered surfaces of the envelope and the flap. With a satisfied little chuckle, she passed over the envelope, pointing to a distinct smudge close to the right-hand edge on the part of the reverse which she had uncovered.

"Found something, eh?" He reached into his case, and extracted a bottle of gray powder and a camel-hair brush. Gently he brushed powder over the area and, taking the magnifying glass in his hand, peered at the irregular print revealed. He shook his head and passed envelope and glass to Susan. "Definitely some kind of print there, but it is too indistinct to be used as evidence."

"Just a minute!" Susan examined the smudge closely. "Look! That definitely looks like the impression of a scar."

Uncle Ted leaned forward for a closer look. "I do believe it is." Carefully he slid the envelope into a larger one taken from his case. "Perhaps not admissible in a court of law, but it might prove useful nevertheless."

Susan looked first at the crudely printed message on the back of the photograph — "HAVE DIAMONDS — WILL SELL BACK $15,000 — WAIT FOR CONTACT." She then gave the picture her attention and methodically examined it. It was black and white, and showed seven large, uncut stones scattered on a sheet of what appeared to be plain brown paper. This paper was in turn on a sheet of newspaper, portions of which were visible at the upper edge and right side of the picture. Again Susan lifted the magnifying glass for closer scrutiny. After two or three minutes she placed the glass carefully on the table and sat back, eyes closed as she concentrated. Her uncle waited patiently; he had witnessed a similar performance many times. He was not surprised when eventually her eyes snapped open, and she rattled off a number of questions.

"Is Mr. Hodge, Mr. Simpson, or Miss Smithers left-handed? Does any of them have a scar on the right thumb? Were the offices searched? Is there a refrigerator in any of the offices? If so, which one? Where . . ."

"Whoa! Whoa!" Uncle Ted laughed as he held up his hand as if to stop a runaway horse. "One question at a time, please! Yes, the secretary is left-handed; I noticed it when she signed her statement. In the same way, I know that both partners are right-handed. Of course, either or both could be ambidextrous, but this I don't know, although in view of your question perhaps I'd better find out. Similarly, I cannot confirm or deny that any of them has a scar on a thumb." He made a note in his book. "Now, what was your next question?"

"Refrigerator."

"No, I don't think so." He pondered for a few seconds. "Of course, I wasn't particularly looking for one, or for a kettle for that matter, but I'm positive that there is one of those because we were offered coffee this morning." He closed his case after replacing his equipment and the photograph. "Why don't we take a stroll back to the office and look?" He grinned broadly at Susan's squeal of delight. That was exactly what she wanted to do, but hadn't dared to ask. Almost at a trot, Susan led the way to the door.

"Good morning again, Miss Smithers." Uncle Ted removed his hat as they entered the outer office. "May I see Mr. Hodge for a few minutes please?"

"No, you may not!" The rather severe looking lady snapped the words, but immediately she was contrite. "I'm so sorry, officer, I didn't mean to be rude. It's just that I'm still upset by the theft."

Uncle Ted was quite right, Susan thought as she noted the slightly bloodshot eyes. The lady had obviously suffered a shock severe enough to reduce her to tears.

"I'm afraid that Mr. Hodge did not feel well, and I insisted that he go home and rest." Miss Smithers sniffed.

"May we have one more glance through his office then, please?" Uncle Ted requested politely, moving to a door to the right as she nodded her consent. He ushered Susan before him.

Susan glanced around the room. It was exactly as she had imagined; thick carpet on the floor, heavy polished wooden desk, with pen set, blotter, and telephone neatly arranged on its surface. Behind was a comfortable looking armchair, and at one end stood an upright chair for the stenographer. Across the office Susan saw a low chesterfield and a coffee table, obviously used to entertain guests and potential customers. Entertain? The word raised another question in her mind. Entertainment implied some sort of refreshment. Susan's eyes continued to wander. In the far corner there was an old-fashioned roll-top desk, out of character with the rest of the room. She walked over to it, and after receiving her uncle's nod of permission, rolled back the top. Inside a hidden light came on, which made a row of expensive cut-glass tumblers sparkle. A lower shelf held bottles, and in one corner there was a small electric ice-making machine, large enough to produce a half dozen ice-cubes at one time. Thoughtfully, Susan closed the top. After peering under the desk and locating an empty wastebasket, she moved to the chesterfield and sat down. She thought hard for several minutes and upon coming to a decision looked up at her uncle.

"I have one more question to ask. When, exactly, did Mr. Hodge return from Montreal?"

"On the midnight flight, last night." He was positive of this fact. The stewardess had confirmed Mr. Hodge's presence on it.

"In that case, I suggest that you immediately obtain a search warrant, and go through his house with a fine-tooth comb."

"And what shall I be searching for?" he asked.

"The negative of the photograph, of course."

"Are you sure?" She had never been wrong on other cases, but this time . . . "We checked his whereabouts. He was definitely on that flight last night."

"I don't dispute that, Uncle, but I'm sure that he's your man. Look, if you're doubtful, check his thumb before you demand to enter the house, and see if he has the scar. But please hurry. He may destroy any evidence there."

That evening Susan could hardly contain her impatience. Frequently she walked across to the window to watch for Uncle Ted's car. She barely touched her dinner. At last her mother complained, "Stop playing with your food, Susan."

Her father smiled. Susan's restlessness was an obvious indication that she was once again involved in her favourite hobby. There was a certain way that she moved about when working on a case with her uncle, and he knew the signs well. "Relax, Susan. He'll be here shortly." He chuckled at her look of surprise. "You don't have to tell me you're into another case with your Uncle Ted." She grinned her confirmation. "Why don't you give us the background before he arrives?"

Once more she went to the window, but no car had magically appeared while her back was turned.

"Okay. It'll help pass the time. Come on, Mum. Leave the dishes; I'll help you afterwards."

With her parents comfortably settled, Susan told them of the events that morning; how she had bumped into Uncle Ted outside the offices of Hodge and Simpson, and how she had persuaded him to tell her all about it over a milk shake in the restaurant. She told them about Mr. Simpson falling ill in the taxi, about Mr. Hodge's trip from California and about the arrival of the envelope containing the photograph. As soon as he saw the photograph with its message, Mr. Hodge showed it to Miss Smithers. They rushed to the safe together; it's in the wall behind his desk, hidden by a large picture. He opened it, but it was she who removed the box and opened the lid. The diamonds weren't there! Right away she called the police, and Uncle Ted responded to the call."

Susan jumped up and rushed to the door as she heard a car crunching the gravel on the driveway. "Was I right? Was I right?" she called to her uncle, not waiting for him to step into the front hall.

"Yes, you were quite right, as usual." He nodded, winking over her head at her father who stood behind her. She sighed with pleasure. "Mr. Hodge is in custody. Now, perhaps I may have a cup of coffee, while you explain your theories?"

Ten minutes later the dishes were washed, Susan helping as she had promised. They were seated around the kitchen table, with Uncle Ted contentedly puffing at his pipe, a cup of coffee in his hand.

"But why were you so convinced that it was Mr. Hodge?" her mother asked.

"There were a number of clues, but most important was the photograph." Her uncle took it from his brief case, and passed it to her mother. "If you look closely, Mum, you can see part of a newspaper at the top of the picture." She leaned over and pointed with her finger. "Under a magnifying glass you can just make out the letters, 'ER, 5, 1978.' Then, lower down, and on the right," — she again pointed — "you can see the last few words of a line, '17 DAYS TO —' and the next line, '— SHOPPERS WILL —'. I think that the date of the newspaper is December 5, 1978, because there are seventeen shopping days to Christmas."

"Why, that's today!" Susan's mother voiced her surprise. "The photograph could only have been taken this morning. But the boy doesn't bring the newspaper until seven o'clock. How could anyone take a photograph of today's paper, and have it delivered through the mail before nine o'clock?"

"That's the point, you see. The letter would have to be in the post office before the last sorting at seven o'clock. I checked, and this is not the same paper as ours; the type is different. I suspected that it was an early edition of a newspaper which may be bought at Montreal

Airport before midnight."

"And, indeed it is," Uncle Ted interjected. "As Susan saw it, Hodge had the opportunity to buy the newspaper, take it home, take the photograph, and mail the letter, all before seven this morning."

"It wasn't surprising that he jumped at the opportunity to go home and rest when Miss Smithson suggested it. He must have spent almost the whole night setting up the photograph and ransom note," Susan's father observed.

"How silly of him to use that particular newspaper," her mother sniffed.

"I'm glad he was silly." Susan smiled at her.

"And from that clue, you figured Mr. Hodge to be the thief?" her father asked.

"Oh no! There were other clues. Look at the printing." She turned over the photograph, picture side downwards. "At first glance it looks like that of a small child, but the words used, and the use of 'HAVE' rather than 'GOT', suggests that it was done by an adult, one who is capable of far neater work. The letters slope backwards, and usually one would think, 'Ah! Left-handed,' but because of the poor way in which the letters are formed I thought it more likely that a right-handed person used his or her left hand to disguise the writing. Uncle Ted told me that Miss Smithers is left-handed, and on that basis I took her off my list of immediate suspects. As far as Mr. Simpson was concerned it really made no difference. He was in hospital from sometime yesterday afternoon, and had no opportunity to prepare the photograph or mail the letter."

"Perhaps the scarred thumb print was the most conclusive piece of evidence, apart from finding the negative of the photograph in Hodge's garbage. At

Susan's urging I obtained a search warrant and rushed out to his house. Hodge opened the front door in answer to our knock, and I held out the warrant almost at eye level. This forced him to raise his hand to take it from me, and I could clearly see the fleshy part of his thumb; there was the scar, just as we had thought."

"Well, I never! Susan Super Sleuth strikes again!" Her father smiled at her proudly.

"But how did he remove the diamonds without his secretary's knowledge? I thought he left for Montreal immediately after he had locked the safe." Her mother was puzzled.

"Hah! That's the clever part. There were no diamonds in the safe in the first place," Uncle Ted answered.

"No diamonds? But the secretary saw them."

"No she didn't, Mother," Susan contradicted. "She *thought* she saw them, but what she *actually* saw were pieces of broken ice cube, which, of course, melted in a few hours. Mr. Hodge carefully staged the accident with the glass of water to provide a logical explanation for the wet cotton batting when the empty box was discovered."

"How did he know that he would not be disturbed when he was preparing the ice cubes? Didn't he run a silly risk there?" her mother asked.

"There was no danger of that. Remember he sent his secretary to buy some aspirin for his headache? This gave him at least four or five minutes to remove an ice cube from the liquor cabinet, smash it into pieces, and lay them on the cotton batting."

"Then there was really no theft at all?" Susan's father asked.

"What did he hope to gain from the charade?" Her mother wrinkled her forehead in question.

"Insurance," Uncle Ted explained. "He expected the photograph to establish automatically the existence of the gems so that, when nothing further was heard from the thief, the insurance company would pay up."

"So it's more of a case of swindle, rather than theft." Susan's father nodded his understanding.

"Right," Susan agreed. "Except that Hodge not only planned to collect from the insurance company, but also to cheat his partner. You see, he really had purchased diamonds worth thirty thousand dollars with funds drawn from the partners' account; he had a signed receipt from a reputable California dealer to prove it. Presumably he planned to dispose of them later and pocket the proceeds."

"Cool customer!" her father exclaimed.

"Yes, and he might well have pulled it off if poor Mr. Simpson had gone to Amsterdam as planned," Susan observed.

"You mean that he would have been the obvious suspect?" her mother asked.

"Yes. He would have found it very difficult to convince anyone that he had not taken the gems, and passed them over to an accomplice in Holland."

"Well, I guess Mr. Hodge has learned something from this: you should take nothing for granted, eh?" Uncle Ted wagged his finger at Susan with a grin. "First rule of detection?"

"Right, Uncle Ted." Susan raised a thumb in agreement.

"I know what I've learned." Her mother paused, ensuring that she had their undivided attention before continuing with a suppressed chuckle, "I've often wondered why the underworld slang for diamonds is 'ice'. Now I know!"